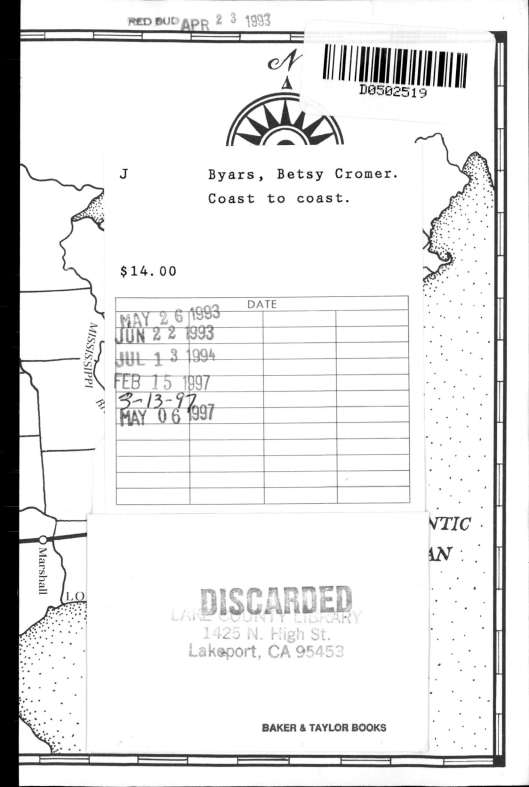

D0502519

J   Byars, Betsy Cromer.
        Coast to coast.

$14.00

DATE		
MAY 2 6 1993		
JUN 2 2 1993		
JUL 1 3 1994		
FEB 15 1997		
3-13-97		
MAY 0 6 1997		

MISSISSIPPI

Marshall

LO

NTIC
AN

BAKER & TAYLOR BOOKS

COAST TO COAST

Also by Betsy Byars

Beans on the Roof
The Night Swimmers
The Animal, the Vegetable, & John D Jones

THE BLOSSOM FAMILY BOOKS

The Not-Just-Anybody Family
The Blossoms Meet the Vulture Lady
The Blossoms and the Green Phantom
A Blossom Promise
Wanted . . . Mud Blossom

COAST
TO COAST

Betsy Byars

**Delacorte
Press**

Published by
Delacorte Press
Bantam Doubleday Dell Publishing Group, Inc.
666 Fifth Avenue
New York, New York 10103

The poem on page 38 is by Emily Dickinson.
The very short excerpts from poems on page 64
are by William Wordsworth, Keith Preston, and
Henry Wadsworth Longfellow respectively.
The longer excerpt of a poem on page 65 is by Robert Browning.
The poem on page 147 is by Edna St. Vincent Millay.

Library of Congress Cataloging in Publication Data

Byars, Betsy Cromer.
Coast to coast / Betsy Byars.
p.   cm.
Summary: Thirteen-year-old Birch encourages her grandfather to
fulfill his dream of flying his old Piper Cub plane from South Carolina
to California and then informs him that she is coming along.
ISBN 0-385-30787-X
[1. Grandfathers—Fiction.   2. Airplanes—Fiction.]   I. Title.
PZ7.B9836Cn   1992
[Fic]—dc20   91-46451
                                                        CIP
                                                         AC

Interior design by Christine Swirnoff

Manufactured in the United States of America

October 1992

10   9   8   7   6   5   4   3   2   1

BVG

to Ed and Harvey

CONTENTS

COAST TO COAST

CHAPTER 1

In the Attic

 BIRCH SAT by the attic window. Motes of dust floated through the sunlight around her.

Ace, the dog, lay at her feet. He panted with the heat. Drops of saliva dotted the dusty floor. He looked up at her and gave a moan of impatience.

"If you're that hot, Ace," she told him absently, "go downstairs." She did not look away from the box in her hands.

The box had once held candy, but now it was bound tightly with an old, faded ribbon. In an attic that had been filled with old things, this box was all that remained.

Birch pulled at the knot, but it had been tied by

someone who did not want the box to be opened. She paused for a moment, caught by an unexpected feeling of unease.

"Birch," her mother called from downstairs.

"What?"

"Come down here, I need you."

"In a minute."

"Is everything out of the attic?"

"Yes."

"Then come help me with the basement."

"I'm coming."

She began to work the ribbon off the box, carefully inching it over the old cardboard. The ribbon slipped off the end of the box and fell in a coil onto the floor. Ace glanced at it with interest, as if waiting for it to do something.

Birch fumbled with the lid, and the box sprang open like something out of a fairy tale.

Sheets of paper, faded and discolored, green, cream, and blue, fluttered from the old lace lining and landed at her feet. Birch bent to gather them up.

She began to read. Shifting through the sheets, she paused to read again. For a moment she sat without moving.

"Oh, Ace. Ace!"

She scrambled to her feet. Clutching the box in both arms, she ran down the attic stairs. The movement caught Ace by surprise and it took him a moment to start after her.

"Mom, guess what?" Birch called as she ran. "Mom, where are you?"

"In the basement."

Birch took the basement stairs two at a time. Her mother was leaning over a card table, marking items for the garage sale. The electric fan, priced at four dollars, turned slowly from side to side, stirring the air.

"You'll never guess what I found."

"I thought you said the attic was clean."

"Mom, this was stuck on a ledge over the window. I didn't see it before. I could have missed it completely! And guess what it is?"

"I can't."

"Mom, it's poems. And this"—she picked up the top sheet—"this is a love poem!" She held out the box. "Mom, these are your mother's old poems. Remember you told me she wrote poetry."

"Yes, but don't bother me with it now, Birch."

"Can I read you this one poem, please?"

"If it's a short one."

"They're all short. Mom, this is going to shock you. Your mother and father were in love. Granny and Pop were in love!"

"Oh, Birch."

"Well, maybe you aren't surprised, but I am. And the poems are all dated. This one's April 1944. Was that before they got married or after?"

Her mother gave it some thought. "Before."

"Here it is." Birch cleared her throat. "Word for word.

> *"Listen, World—*
> *Listen, Sea—*
> *Listen, all the powers that be.*
> *Earl loves me.*

"Whoo," Birch said, "I didn't know Granny had it in her. You want to hear another one."

"Maybe later."

"One more quickie. This is dated May 1944. The romance is heating up.

> *"Of all the treasures*
> *In the world,*
> *Like the oyster*
> *With its pearl*
> *I have Earl.*

"Where's Pop? I have to read these to him. To be honest I never thought of Pop as a treasure of the world."

"Pop's at the airport."

"When's he going to get home?"

"He'll be here for lunch."

"Mom, do you think he knows about these?"

"Your grandfather was never much for poetry. It embarrassed him."

"So can I have them? The poems?"

"I think your grandmother would want you to have them. You probably got your gift for poetry from her. But you have to check with Pop first. All of these things are his."

"I understand. I will buy them at the garage sale if I have to."

Birch sat down on the basement steps. There was a startled yelp from Ace. "Well, if you don't want to get sat on," she told him, "you shouldn't lie down under people."

She brushed off the back of her legs. "Sitting on Ace is like sitting on a porcupine."

"I wouldn't know," her mother commented idly.

Birch sat down, beside Ace this time. She rubbed him behind his stubby ears.

"I got the poems out of order when I dropped them," she told her mom. She began to sort through the sheets of paper.

"I need some help, Birch." Birch could tell that her mom was losing patience.

"I'll help just as soon as I get these straightened out—" She broke off. "Oh, Mom! Guess what? Here's one dated, June twelve. My birthday. She wrote a poem when I was born! A birth poem! 'For the Newborn.' I guess you hadn't named me yet."

She read the brief lines to herself. She read them again. Her smile faded.

"This doesn't make sense."

"What?"

Birch bent over the pale paper and read the thin,

spidery blue script one more time. She felt a chill at the back of her neck.

> *The baby took one fluttering gasp*
> *Two . . .*
> *Three . . .*
> *Each softer than the last.*
> *Four . . .*
> *One more. . . .*
> *Passed. All past.*

"So, read me the poem."

"No, it's nothing . . . nothing. I thought it was my birth poem, but I was wrong. It's more like, I don't know"—she choked on the words—"a death one."

"More like what? I didn't hear you."

"Nothing."

Birch held the sheet of paper gingerly, by one corner. It trembled as the electric fan turned in her direction.

"Read it to me. I want to hear it."

"I'm having a problem making it out—it's blue ink on blue paper."

She felt as if she were on the edge of some knowledge that she didn't want, maybe that she couldn't handle.

"You've got me interested," her mother continued.

"I've already put it on the bottom of the pile. Anyway, Mom, it'll make you cry."

"It's that sad?"

"No, everything makes you cry. I saw you weeping over two pillows yesterday."

"Oh, Birch, those were your grandmother's pillows when she was a girl. Their names were Willow and Billow."

"She named pillows?"

"Yes. Oh, I'm going to start crying again if I'm not careful."

Birch lifted her head. "Oh, there's Pop, home from the airport."

She jumped to her feet. And Ace, hearing the sound of the truck, ran on his short legs for the garage.

"Mom, don't tell Pop about the poems yet. Let me do it."

"All right."

"I want to wait until he's not so worried about his plane."

"Birch, where are you going now?"

"Just upstairs. I don't want the poems to get mixed in with the sale junk. I'll be right back."

Clutching the box against her pounding heart, Birch turned and ran up the stairs.

CHAPTER 2

Secret Missions

 "Talk to me, Pop," Birch said.

"I don't come out to the airport to have conversations," her grandfather answered mildly. "If you wanted to talk, you should have stayed home with your mom. She's the talker."

Birch was sitting on a bench in front of the T hangar, nervously swinging her bare feet back and forth. Her grandfather was getting ready to wash his airplane.

"I had to get out of the house. I used to love to come to your house when it was your house, but now —with everything gone, it's, I don't know—spooky."

Birch and Pop had been at the airport for an hour,

but Birch had not mentioned the box of poems she had found in the attic that morning.

"Oh, I know something I haven't told you." Her words came in a rush as if this afternoon was going to turn out wrong, and she had to hurry through it. "Guess how I found out I was named for a tree? You'll love this.

"It was my first day of kindergarten, Pop. My teacher, Miss Penny, goes, 'Birch, what a lovely name.' My mom goes, 'I named her for a tree.'

"Everyone started giggling. Miss Penny goes, 'Quiet, boys and girls, there is nothing funny about being named for a tree.'

"I just stood there, saying I ain't believing this. I was named for a tree.

"At recess, this snob named Priscilla goes, 'You were named for a tree-eee,' like that. When my mom picked me up I burst out crying—the only time I cry is when I'm mad. 'Why did you name me for a tree? Everybody's teasing me about it.' My mom goes, 'Who, exactly, is teasing you?' I go, 'Priscilla.' My mom goes, 'You know what a priscilla is, don't you? A pris-cilla is a curtain. Would you rather be named for a beautiful tree or a curtain?'

"The next day when Priscilla goes, 'We don't want to play with you. You were named for a tree-eee.' I go, 'Well, you were named for a curtain. Who wants to play with a curtain. Come on, you guys, we don't want to play with a curtain.'

"That's how I became popular in kindergarten—by making everybody scared of me."

"There's nicer ways to become popular."

"I suppose. Now it's your turn to pick what to talk about."

He hesitated.

"There must be something you haven't told me—maybe something about when I was little. When I was born, maybe." She watched her grandfather intently.

"I know what I want to talk about. I don't want to get rid of this airplane. That's what I want to talk about!"

"Oh," she said.

"I want to get rid of the house. I'm rattling around in there by myself. I don't want the furniture." He laid one hand on the prop of the J-3 Cub. "But I mind selling my airplane."

"Why don't you take your airplane with you? There must be retirement homes that allow airplanes."

Her grandfather shook his head. "It was hard enough to find one that would take Ace." His intensity was gone as quickly as it had come.

"You can help me wash the plane if you want to," Pop offered. "First we'll hose it off."

"At last, some action." Birch took one of the old bath towels.

"Now don't press hard on the fabric. It's just cotton cloth with a few coats of paint."

"I won't."

10

"And don't worry about the top of the wing. I'll get that with the ladder."

Birch sighed. "Pop, I'm not a child. I'm thirteen. You're just like Mom. If Mom wants me to make a salad, she goes, 'Walk to the refrigerator. Open the door. Reach down. Open the crisper. Take out the lettuce. Walk with the lettuce to the counter . . .' " She trailed off, then added in a different voice, "But she doesn't always tell me important things."

Her grandfather didn't respond. She watched as he hosed down the plane. Then she dipped her towel into the soapy water and began wiping the yellow fabric.

"I want it to look good when the man comes to get it day after tomorrow," he said.

"It will, Pop . . . but, listen, when you were young, did your parents keep things from you?"

"Like what?"

"I don't know, just things."

He pulled back to look at his airplane. It was a small high-wing plane with two seats, one behind the other. "You know, a Piper J-3 Cub was the first thing I ever wanted out of life."

"I can't remember the first thing I wanted."

"I was sixteen, and all my life people had been telling me I couldn't leave one place or another. I couldn't leave the yard. I couldn't leave the house. I couldn't leave the field until five o'clock. I cut tobacco in those days."

"I didn't know that, Pop."

11

"So I was sixteen and it had just hit me that it was going to be like that the rest of my life. I was bent over cutting tobacco with a knife—that's about the hardest work there is. My head was down around my knees, sweat was pouring off me, my back was breaking, and I straightened up and saw a yellow airplane in the sky. It might as well have been pulling a banner saying FREEDOM. I wanted to be up in that airplane as bad as I ever wanted anything in my life."

Birch's eyes were on her grandfather, his on the invisible freedom banner. For once, she let the silence stand.

"On Sunday, I hitchhiked to the airport, found out lessons were ten dollars an hour, and hitchhiked home."

"You didn't get to take flying lessons?"

"Birch, back then if I had two quarters to rub together, I was rich."

He moved to the other side of the plane. Birch followed. "I knew you were poor, but not that poor."

"I had one hope. There was a radio show back then called 'Wings of Destiny.' It was sponsored by Wings cigarettes. Every week they gave away a J-3, and a uniformed pilot named Arthur Segar Pierce would deliver it."

"Did you win?"

"No. To win you had to send in a coupon out of a pack of Wings and I didn't smoke. I learned my flying in the war,"—Pop rested his freckled hand on the plane—"in a J-3 just like this one."

"This is getting off the subject," Birch said. Her mind kept flicking back to that moment in the attic when she had held the unopened box and felt the first stirrings of unease. And, later, the poem—an arrow pointing to something she dreaded to see, yet had to follow. "But do you happen to remember the day I was born?"

He paused, trying to make the connection. "June twelve, wasn't it?"

As he said the date, Birch saw it as it had been written on the bottom of that sheet of old blue paper. She felt from now on she would always see it that way, even on calendars.

"I know the date, Pop. I want details, like, oh, were there any problems? Did I have a hard time breathing?"

"No, you were as big and healthy as they come—weighed eight or nine pounds."

"Nine. But did I, you know, stop breathing?"

"Who told you that?"

"Nobody." Birch felt she was getting too close to that invisible edge. She pulled back. "Tell me a funny flying story, Pop."

"Let's see. Well, I flew a J-3 in the war."

"That's funny?"

Her grandfather turned the nozzle of the hose, and the water changed to a fine mist.

"I was what they called a grasshopper pilot. We took off and landed anywhere. I dropped supplies to patrols in the jungle, I delivered blood plasma to the wounded, I spotted for the artillary. One time I flew Bob Hope to entertain the troops.''

"The Bob Hope?''

Pop nodded. He picked up two dry towels and threw one to Birch. Together they began drying the yellow fabric of the fuselage.

"Now this plane,'' he said, "I bought this plane ten years ago. My partner—Dwane Hicks—and me were going to fly it across the country, coast to coast.''

"What happened?''

"Oh, first Dwane moved to Florida. Then your grandmother got cancer, and I had to look after her.''

"You could still go.''

"Time's run out.''

"If I wanted to go as bad as you do, I'd go. I wouldn't let anything stop me.'' She gave him a narrow look. "You know what?''

"What?''

"You're probably smart to go to a nursing home.''

He drew back as if stung. "Retirement home!''

"Whatever. You used to go, 'Life's an adventure, Birch.' You used to make it an adventure. The best thing about you and me was our secret missions. You'd say, 'Birch and I are off on a secret mission.' ''

Those days seemed so far away that she felt tears sting her eyes.

"I used to love our secret missions,'' she went on. "One time you took me to the old Charleston museum. I was real little. There was a mummy in a case, and you showed me a way to sneak my hand under

14

the back of the case and touch the mummy. I was so impressed. I was the only person in my play group at Kiddie Kollege who had touched a mummy."

"Well, I touched it too," he said stubbornly.

"Yes, but you weren't in my play group." She grinned and then sighed.

"Now you're through with things like that, Pop. If a secret mission came along right this minute, you'd go, 'No, I'm too old for secret missions.' "

She looked away.

"I guess all the good times are over."

CHAPTER 3

Kick the Tire, Twang the Wire

 BIRCH'S GRANDFATHER turned abruptly to watch a Cessna coming in for a landing. Even after the white wings had disappeared behind the hangar, he kept his face turned away. His neck had reddened.

"I'm sorry I said that—about you getting old."

He didn't answer.

"Pop, I don't even know why I said it. I've got things on my mind and I know that's no excuse but . . ."

Birch kept watching him, looking for a sign that her apology was taking effect.

"Pop, don't give me the silent treatment. You know I can't stand it."

Pop turned with a sigh.

16

She continued in the same nervous way. "You know who gives me the silent treatment all the time? Mrs. Bumgardner. That's Dad's receptionist. See, every time I do something wrong, I have to go down to Dad's office to have a talk. And I sit there with all the little kids waiting to have their teeth straightened, and I go, 'Mrs. Bumgardner, do you know what I did wrong?' She puts one finger to her lips. I hate that. I go, 'I honestly don't know what I did!' One little kid got so interested he said, 'When you find out what you did, let me know, all right?' "

Birch fell silent. She wouldn't mind being in that waiting room right now. She would go in and have a serious, office-type talk with her dad. She knew she couldn't talk to her mom. Her mom was too emotional.

Birch straightened. "Hey, I've got an idea—one final secret mission," she said. "Let's go up."

Pop's expression did not change. When he was hurt, he looked like something carved from stone.

"I'm serious," Birch said, putting more enthusiasm into her voice. "I really want to go up, don't you?"

He gave his head a shake, the way a horse shakes off a troublesome fly.

"Why not? You wanted to go up yesterday. You offered to fly me over the beach, remember?"

Again he shook his head.

"Why are you shaking your head? Because you don't remember or because—"

"You don't want to go." His smile was tight.

17

"I do. I want to do something. I can't explain it. I have to do something. And here is this perfectly good airplane."

His jaws moved, chewing on the idea.

"What I meant about getting old, Pop, was that it's not getting pain in your joints or bad teeth. It's, like, not wanting to have fun."

Her grandfather got busy. He emptied the bucket and put the wet towels inside. "Help me push the plane back in the hangar. I'm tired of talking about my age."

"Yes, but it's my turn to pick. Remember? I picked being named for a tree, you picked flying in the war, now I pick this. I want to talk about you."

"Birch, the airplane is sold."

"You haven't got the money yet."

"I don't want to take any chances."

"See? Don't take any chances—that's exactly what getting old is. Don't step on the grass. Don't go out of the yard!"

"That's enough. I mean it."

Birch was silent for a moment. Then in a different voice, as if she were taking up a new topic, she said, "You never have taken me up."

Her grandfather glanced at the sky. Beneath her eyeshade, Birch's eyes narrowed. She knew she had him now.

"I really want to go!" As she said it, she realized it was true. She needed to get away from this world, and this was the way to do it. "What are we waiting for?"

"I don't guess it would hurt to fly to the beach and back."

"Then get in! Let's go!"

"Don't get in too big a hurry." Her grandfather smiled. It was his first real smile of the afternoon.

Birch followed him around the plane. "What are you doing?"

"Well, right now, I'm doing a preflight inspection. I check the tires, the control surfaces, move them for freedom and cable looseness." He raised the aileron and looked at the cable underneath. "I check the tail wheel springs . . . the stabilizer trim . . ."

"Does everybody do this? Or are you just extra careful?"

"There used to be a saying. 'Kick the tire. Twang the wire. Light the fire and let her go.' Nowadays a pilot checks everything—the prop for nicks, the cowling pins for security . . ." He moved around the plane. "Look under the cowl—birds are very fond of building nests under cowls. Check the oil—the gas. The gas cap's up here."

"What's that wire sticking out of it?"

Pop unscrewed the cap. "That's the gas gauge. See, there's a cork on the end. The cork floats on the gas, and as the gas goes down, so does the cork and the wire."

Pop reached in the cabin and removed a clear plastic tube from the seat pocket. He drained some gas into the tube, checked it and threw it out. "Good! No water got in the gas from our wash job."

"How do you know, Pop?"

"Water's heavier than gas, so it would be on the bottom. And they look different."

"So can I get in now?" He nodded, and Birch stepped to the right side of the plane. "Do I sit in the front or back?"

"The pilot sits in the back."

"But how do you see the instruments?"

"I can see all I have to. Put your foot on the tire, not on the strut and . . ."

Birch pulled herself in and fastened the seat belt. "This is the first time I've been in a little airplane. Pop, your instruments are ancient."

"They're 1940, same as the plane." Her grandfather leaned into the cockpit. "This is the altimeter—it tells you how high you are. I'm setting that to the altitude of the field—it's about sea level so I set it on zero. Carburetor heat—off. Switch—off."

He moved the stick back and forth while looking at the tail, then from side to side while watching the wing. "Put your heels on the brake pedals."

"Oh, we both have brake pedals?"

"Yes, it's dual control."

She looked down at the pedals and positioned her feet so that her heels were on the smaller ones.

"I'm going to swing the prop to start the engine."

"You mean, like, it's going to start and I'm going to be sitting in here by myself with the engine going?"

20

Pop opened the throttle a half inch.

"Look at my feet, Pop, and make sure they're on the brakes."

"I did."

"Because I do not want to take off by myself. I saw that in an Abbott and Costello movie."

"This is the gas primer." Pop pulled out a knob and slowly pushed it back in. Then he stepped to the front of the plane and gave the prop a few turns. Birch listened to the clicks and watched the tip of the prop over the cowling.

"Now turn that overhead ignition switch on for me."

"This?"

"Right, and yell 'Contact' just before you do."

"Incidentally, I'm terrified. Contact!"

"Brakes?"

"Brakes!" she yelled, pressing her heels harder.

Pop came around and stood by the cabin. He reached forward with his right hand and gave the prop a quick downward pull. The engine caught. Pop leaned in and pushed the throttle back. The propeller turned slowly at idle, almost invisible against the blue sky.

Then he climbed in. "I got the brakes now," he yelled above the noise of the engine.

Birch took her feet off the pedals. "I feel a lot better with you in here."

The plane started forward. Following the yellow line on the pavement, they moved from the ramp down the taxiway and stopped just short of the runway.

"I'm revving up the engine now to check the magnetos and carburetor heat."

"Check everything!"

He leaned forward. "Belt tight?"

"You bet. Let's go!"

"Birch?"

"What, Pop?"

"Let's don't say anything about this to your mom."

"Of course not! It's a secret mission." She put one hand on the window. "Aren't you going to close this?"

"We can close it later if you get too much wind."

"No, I like it open! Let's go!" And Birch's heart raced as Pop turned the J-3 onto runway nine.

CHAPTER 4

The Missing Piece

 WIND RUSHED around Birch, whipping her hair from her face. The noise was terrible. She grabbed the steel bar above the instrument panel with one hand, her visor with the other.

The J-3 picked up speed.

Birch glanced out the window over the side of the plane. The gray concrete runway flashed by below. The right tire spun as it left the ground.

"We're up!" she yelled. The J-3 lifted smoothly into the air. Birch took a deep breath. The sound of the engine roared in her ears. She could feel its throb beneath her feet.

The thrill of the air overtook her and for the first

time she forgot the sickening jolt of the birth poem she had read that morning.

The wings wavered as the plane hit an air current. Birch gasped, but the ride was already smooth again.

"I like it, Pop!" she yelled over her shoulder.

She looked down. They were still climbing, leaving the airport behind. They passed over the Stono River, then the ribbed fields of open farmland. She could see the ocean beyond.

"Let's don't go home yet. Let's just keep riding— let's go all the way down the coast."

"We'd end up in Florida."

"Fine with me!"

Pop turned south at the coast, and the bright sun blazed across the windshield. "I'll level off at a thousand feet," he said. Birch heard the engine grow quieter as he throttled back.

The ocean was on one side, the wide Carolina beach on the other. Birch breathed the fresh salt air. People were on the sand with bright sun umbrellas, yellow rafts, striped towels. Swimmers kept to the shoreline. Two bicycles moved up the beach.

"You can see everything from up here!" Birch said.

She rested her arm on the side of the plane. It gave her a sporty, racy feeling. Her visor fluttered in the wind.

Her grandfather pointed. "Shrimp boats, and that's Kiawah Island. Look at the size of those houses!"

She nodded. "Those people may be rich, but they don't have airplanes. If they did, they'd be up here!"

Pop smiled.

Birch felt as if this was her first flight. She had flown on airliners, but there had been no contact with the wind or the ground. She might as well have been in a sealed room.

And the view from the jet—the tiny towns, the almost invisible roads, the snakelike rivers—had given her no feeling of height, no feeling of being way up there, just a feeling of remoteness. The airline pilot had said, "We're level at thirty thousand feet," but even that had not been impressive.

Now with the wind in her face and the roar of the engine in her ears, at one thousand feet above the ground, she was all of a sudden way up there in a way she had never been before.

Some children on the beach looked up and waved. Pop wagged his wings back at them.

"I love it!" she said over her shoulder.

"You want to try?"

"Is it legal?"

"Sure, I'm the pilot in command."

She reached for the stick, then hesitated. "I'm afraid," she admitted. "I don't want to make us crash."

"I'm not going to let you get into trouble. Hold the stick. I've got it too."

She wrapped her fingers around the control stick.

"You want to go left or right?" he asked.

Birch nodded toward shore.

"Push the stick to the right and see what happens."

She put a little pressure on the stick, and the right wing dipped. The J-3 banked toward the beach. She felt her grandfather put a little opposite pressure. The wings gently came back parallel to the horizon.

"Can I try that the other way?"

"Go ahead."

"I like this," she yelled. "I could go all over the sky like this." She turned to the left, then to the right. "Can I go up a little higher?"

"Pull back on the stick."

She pulled back and gasped as the plane rose. "Climbing's scary. I can't see. You take it."

Her grandfather took the stick. "Now we're level at fifteen hundred feet."

"I'm ready to try again, Pop. I got my guts back."

Birch flew until her grandfather finally said, "Have you had enough flying for one day?"

"No way."

She heard the boom of his laughter over the roar of the engine.

"I don't want to go back, Pop."

"Well, we better head back anyway. Your mom's going to be wondering where we are. You got any idea where the airport is?"

Birch glanced over her shoulder. "Back that way."

"That's north. Check the compass."

"Where is it?" She glanced over the panel. "Is it one of the instruments with a little bear cub in the middle?"

Her grandfather stuck his arm over her shoulder and pointed to a circular instrument.

"North is N, so turn the plane around till the compass is on N."

"Don't help me now."

Birch pushed the stick to the left and made a 180 degree turn. The numbers slipped around behind the thick glass. She could feel her grandfather's hand helping her. "I can do it by myself!" she said. Then she headed up the coast. "See?"

"You want to land or you want me to?" her grandfather asked when the airport was in sight.

"Well, I'll let you do that."

Her grandfather pointed to the faded orange windsock. "Wind's shifted. We'll go in on runway three."

Birch looked over the side as her grandfather throttled all the way back. The J-3 floated along, sinking easily. The prop swished around at idle.

There was a green field below with brown cows and white seagulls. As the plane passed over, the gulls lifted into the air and turned to the sea.

Ahead stretched the runway. A plane was taking off. It was startlingly white against the blue sky.

There was a long moment when the J-3 seemed to hang over the earth, trying not to land. Then it settled on the runway and, with a squeak of the tires, slowed to a stop.

Her grandfather taxied to the hangar.

"Oh, I really liked it, Pop," Birch said, as she climbed out. "You know, I felt very in touch with the ground, and that's funny because I wasn't touching it at all."

As they pushed the J-3 back in the hangar, she said, "I'm beginning to think I could learn to fly, Pop. Maybe I inherited the flying gene."

"You could learn if you wanted to."

"It doesn't seem that hard."

"That's what the Cub was designed for—to make people think it's not that hard." He smiled. "The Cub's a trainer. Piper made it to give flying lessons in. Watch the wingtip."

"I am. You've got plenty of room. I can't wait to tell my friends. Except, guess what? I'm not speaking to my three best friends, Pop. You know what they did to me? We were going in this movie—*Robin Hood*—and there's this cute boy named David? And he was going in with his friends. Brenda knows I like David, so she goes, 'Let's sit by them.' We watch where they sit and we follow. I go in first so I can end up sitting by David. Then, you know what my three best friends did, Pop? They slipped back and sat somewhere else. I sit by David and I look around and they're gone! Pop, I was so embarrassed I just got up and left."

Pop was standing back from the plane, watching it. Birch could see that he hadn't heard a word she'd said.

"Flying like we were doing—just for the fun of flying—that's freedom, that's what I was talking about."

He seemed exhilarated by the flight. His cheeks were pink. His eyes shone.

28

"Yes, I really do see what you were talking about."

"I'm going to miss this. You know, Birch, your grandmother did jigsaw puzzles. She was always working on one, and every now and then, there'd be a piece missing. And the missing piece was all that mattered to her. The whole rest of the puzzle was nothing. That's the way I am about flying. For the rest of my life, it'll be the missing piece."

With his words, the chill of the birth poem fell over her. The missing piece . . . She knew what it was to have one of those.

"Maybe we can fly tomorrow, Birch. Maybe go someplace special . . ."

She glanced at her grandfather as he broke off. The look of excitement was fading. He was on his way to being an old man again.

He turned without a word and headed for the parking lot. He opened the truck door and slid into the driver's seat. It was as if he had forgotten Birch was there.

"Are we going home already?"

He slammed the door.

"Pop, let's don't go home yet. Please. I—well, don't leave me!"

She ran to the truck and climbed in.

In the silence that followed, Birch said, "Listen, if you're serious about going somewhere special, I'll go. I'll go anywhere you want to."

"The plane's sold."

"But—"

He cut her off with a shake of his head. Then he backed out of the parking space and headed for home.

CHAPTER 5

Eight Maps Wide

 ACE WAS STANDING in the middle of the driveway, watching for the truck. When the truck turned in, he began to bark.

He worked his way to the driver's side, where Pop would get out. His barks lowered to a growl. He crouched.

Pop cracked the door. "Calm down, Ace," he said. "I couldn't take you. You weren't around."

"Ace is not very bright," Birch said. "He thinks it's your shoes that are responsible for taking you away. He's waiting to attack your shoes. Like, wow, I'm gonna to make these shoes sorry."

"Ace knows. He just can't bring himself to attack

31

me. Once a dog has been abandoned, like Ace, you
have to forgive him for attacking shoes."

Pop sighed tiredly as he stepped down from the
truck. At once Ace pounced on his left shoe. Pop went
down to the basement, shaking the dog off.

"That's enough now, Ace, let up."

Pop paused to look at a box on the miscellaneous
table and Birch ran up the steps. "Mom! Guess what!"

"Where's your grandfather?"

"Downstairs. Mom, guess what! I flew Pop's plane."

"What's he doing in the basement?"

"Looking at a box of papers. You didn't let me finish. I flew, Mom! I flew! I piloted the plane! I didn't
want to come down!"

"Did you ask Pop about the poems?"

The good feeling left Birch. "No."

"Why not?"

Birch shrugged. "It wasn't the right time."

"I thought you absolutely couldn't wait."

Again, Birch shrugged.

"Well, you cannot take the poems without asking
him."

"Maybe I don't want them after all."

Her mother watched her for a moment. Birch
thought her mother was—at last—going to ask what
was wrong.

"Birch," she began, but Pop interrupted.

Pushing open the kitchen door, he cut between
them on his way to the table.

Pop set a cardboard box down and pulled up a chair. He lifted a map from the box and unfolded it.

"Oh, Pop, I'm glad you're back. I found a cigar box full of coins. Some may be valuable."

"Sell them . . . sell everything."

"I can't put a price on them without knowing what they're worth." She waited, then sighed. "Is it all right if I divide them up for the grandchildren?"

"That'll be fine."

"Did you have time to look at the tools while you were downstairs? I know you won't need the lawn-mower and the gardening things, but you ought to keep a set of tools. Even in a retirement community there'll be times when you'll need a hammer or a screwdriver."

"All right, I'll keep some. Just don't bother me right now."

"When? After supper?"

"Yes, if you'll let me alone."

She turned swiftly, pushed open the swinging door with both hands and went into the dining room. "Birch, will you come in here for a minute?" she called.

Birch followed and stood with her back against the door, her arms crossed. She had had a lot of happy meals in this room, but now the table was piled with boxes of things her mother was keeping, and the pictures were down from the wall.

She took a deep breath to prepare herself for her mother's question.

"Birch, I need your help."

"What?"

"I need your help with Pop. You see what he's doing in there, don't you?"

"What?"

"Looking at maps—aviation maps. He's going to be
poring over them all night. I know the man. Please
see if you can get him to go down and look at the
tools." She ran her hands through her hair.

"Mom, if he doesn't want to look at tools, he
shouldn't have to look at tools."

"He doesn't want to look at anything—tools, books,
you name it—he doesn't want to look at it. He begged
me to come down here, begged me, and get rid of
things for him, and now he won't help me."

"He just wants his airplane!"

"Birch, this is my whole girlhood." She made a ges-
ture that took in the entire house. "This is my life. I
am throwing away my life, and he won't even look at
a few measly tools."

"Mom, please don't cry."

"I can't help it. I'm tired. If he would have waited
one month, your dad could have come to help me,
and I wouldn't be falling apart every five minutes,
but, oh, no, it had to be done right now."

"So, what do you want me to do? I remember—
look at tools."

She pushed open the swinging doors to the
kitchen. "Want to go downstairs and look at the tools,
Pop?"

34

"No."

"I don't either, but I think we're going to have to."

"I'm busy."

He adjusted his glasses and pulled his nose. He always did this when he was deep in thought. He peered closer at a map. He marked a spot with one finger, and then he moved his hand across the sheet of paper to another spot.

"What are you doing, Pop?"

"Looking at maps. Don't bother me."

Birch came closer and leaned over his shoulder.

"Your mother was going to sell my box of maps," he said. "These are the maps Dwane and I marked our route on. Remember I told you we were going to fly coast to coast? You mom was selling this whole box of maps for fifty cents."

"That's why she wants you to go through stuff."

Birch leaned over the map, looking curiously at the pale green expanse of low country, the yellow cities, blue lakes and curling rivers, the blue and magenta keyhole shaped lines around some of the airports. Across the map was the slash of red magic marker.

"Show me where we went today," she said.

"Well, here's the John's Island airport." He put his index finger on a magenta circle. "We took off on runway nine, this one. Remember seeing a nine?"

"Yes."

"That nine stands for ninety—ninety degrees. That means that when we took off, our heading was ninety degrees—due east. We went over the Stono River and turned south at the coast. Right about here, you turned us around and we came north to the airport."

"I always wondered what those numbers on the end of the runway stood for."

"Now you know. If your runway's twenty-seven, your heading's two hundred and seventy degrees— due west. If your runway's three, your heading's thirty degrees."

"That's neat. Is this magic marker line your route to California?"

"Yes, we were going to head west toward Atlanta, stopping at Allendale . . . Berry Hill . . . Louisville, Georgia. Just past Atlanta we'd meet up with Interstate Twenty and follow it."

His finger went off the map. He reached in the box for the next one. Birch waited while he spread it out.

"We'd pass over the Mississippi River at Vicksburg, hit Texas, still on I-Twenty . . . Wait a minute, I'll get the next map."

As he unfolded it, he said, "We were going to land at little airports where we could get car gas. It's cheaper. Here we are—we'd go south of Dallas—" He broke off. "I'll spread them all out so you can see."

He pushed his chair back from the table and knelt on the floor. He began laying out the maps, spreading them with his long hands, shifting them until the red line stretched from the kitchen table to the door of the dining room, across eight maps.

"We only use the tip of this map . . . Tucson . . . Blythe—that's where we'd cross into California . . ."

Birch could see the vision in his eyes. She dropped onto her knees beside him. "Pop!"

"We hadn't decided for sure where we'd cross the San Gabriel Mountains . . . probably along about here—"

"Pop!" Birch glanced in the direction of the dining room and lowered her voice to a whisper. "Are you thinking what I'm thinking?"

His jaw set like concrete. "I'm not thinking about anything but where me and Dwane were going to cross the San Gabriels."

"Yes, you are too. You're thinking about flying to California—probably tomorrow."

"I am not," he said, childlike.

"You are too!"

"Well, maybe the thought flitted into my mind. When you get my age, you don't think sensibly all the time. But there's no way I can do it."

"Why?"

"For one thing, I sold the airplane."

"You didn't get the money."

"Birch, I want to look at these maps in peace. I don't want to look at tools and books and I don't want to listen to your foolishness. All right?"

"I will disappear into the living room."

"Don't you go in there and tell your mom I'm going to the Pacific Ocean. She's making my life miserable enough as it is."

"I'm not going to tell her anything. She makes me miserable sometimes too. But, Pop, before I go, can I say one thing?"

"What?"

She swallowed. "I came across a box of Granny's poems today. And so—so ever since then I've been thinking about poetry, and life, and all. And . . ."

She paused. He waited.

"And a lot of times I don't understand poetry."

Still he waited.

"There are even courses that help you to understand poetry, which I haven't taken yet."

A slight frown of puzzlement creased his brow.

"But I just thought of this one poem and I do understand it. It's by Emily Dickinson."

She held one hand over her heart. She swallowed. "I gave a report on her in Poetry Club. That's how I know this poem.

> *"We never know how high we are*
> *Till we are called to rise;*
> *And then, if we are true to plan,*
> *Our statures touch the skies."*

She watched for his reaction. When there was none, she stepped forward. "Don't you get it?"

He sat bewildered in his sea of maps. He shook his head.

"Pop, this is what it means. It means that we—you

and me—*we* are called to rise. It means that our statures—yours and mine—*our* statures are going to touch the skies. It means, Pop, that you are going to California and I am going with you!''

CHAPTER 6

===

Showdown at Midnight

 BIRCH SAT in the bathroom, on the edge of the bathtub. She stared at the air in front of her. The box of poems lay on her lap.

Her grandfather's house was quiet, but the kitchen light was still on. Its reflected glow lit up the bathroom window. An occasional moth fluttered against the screen.

After the excitement of thinking she and Pop were on their way to California had come the letdown, that final, "That's enough! And hush about it!"

She felt now that going to California would have been her salvation. She could have looked at whatever it was from a comfortable distance, the way she had looked down at the earth that afternoon.

Now all she had were these poems. She opened the box and lifted one of the sheets of paper. At the top of the page, the thin spidery handwriting read "For Earl."

> *If I could have written*
> *My poems in the sky—*
> *White on blue*
> *Letter by letter*
> *Would you have looked up*
> *And liked them better?*

Birch let the poem fall back into the box, as if it were heavy. She closed the lid. Slowly she worked the ribbon back into place.

She had not read the birth poem since morning. It was still on the bottom of the pile. But its powerful effect lingered, giving her the feeling that it marked the end of something—her carefree girlhood, perhaps.

She repeated the poem to herself, moving her lips as she remembered the words.

> *The baby took one fluttering gasp*
> *Two . . .*
> *Three . . .*
> *Each softer than the last.*
> *Four . . .*
> *One more . . .*
> *Passed. All past.*

The last line echoed in her brain.

Suddenly the bathroom door opened.

"Birch, what are you doing sitting there in the dark?"

"Mom! I'm not in the dark. I can see from the window."

"Are you still poring over those poems?"

"No! Well, yes, I can't seem to stop. I want to, Mom, because they're sad, a lot of them, but I get back in bed and I keep thinking about them."

"Those poems . . ." Her mother paused.

"Birch, those poems were your grandmother's thoughts. You're looking at her thoughts. That was how she expressed herself. And in the course of her life, she had sad thoughts like everybody else. I've had about a hundred and fifty sad thoughts in the past week, if you want to know the truth, only I didn't write them down on a piece of paper for my grandchildren to worry over. Now come back to bed."

"Just let me—"

"Come—to—bed."

Birch followed her back to the bedroom they were sharing. This had been her mother's room when she was a girl. Birch lay down in the twin bed. She gave the top sheet a shake. The sheet billowed and then settled lightly on her tense body.

Thoughts rolled around and around in Birch's mind. Sleep was impossible. She wanted to fly out of this bed and away from her thoughts. And Pop could help her do that . . . Only he wouldn't.

She turned over so roughly that the bed springs rattled.

It had been especially painful to watch Pop folding up his maps after supper, putting them back in the box, lowering the lid as if it were the lid on his own coffin. And hers!

She threw back the sheet and came up on one elbow. She slung her feet over the side of the bed and, watching her mother in the opposite twin bed, felt for her sandals. Her mother did not move, and Birch slid her feet into her shoes and quietly crossed the room.

She was at the door when her mother lifted her head. "Birch, where are you going now?"

"Nowhere, Mom, just downstairs for a minute. I've got to tell Pop something."

"Dad's asleep."

"No, he isn't. The kitchen light's still on."

Her mother clicked on the bedside lamp and looked at her watch. "Birch, it's twelve-fifteen. I have got to get some sleep. The garage sale is in the morning, and people are going to start coming at dawn. Get back in bed."

"I have to tell Pop something, Mom. It's important. I'll be right back."

"Birch—"

"Mom, I have to!"

"Then tell him whatever you've got to tell him and come back to bed." Her mom snapped off the light with such force that the lamp rocked in place.

"Thanks."

43

Birch ran down the long staircase. The pictures had been removed from the wall, and the pale rectangles where they had hung gave the stairway a ghostly look.

She pushed open the kitchen door. "Pop?"

He didn't hear her. He was dialing the telephone, then waiting for an answer. Ace lay under the table, at Pop's feet. Ace lifted his head and yawned. When he saw it was Birch, he dropped his head back between Pop's shoes.

Birch watched Pop from the doorway. He didn't look pitiful now. He adjusted the notepad in front of him and wagged a pencil impatiently between his fingers.

Birch gave him a curious look. Silently she let the door close behind her.

Her grandfather spoke into the phone. "This is Piper three oh three six two. I'm departing John's Island at thirteen hundred zulu, going to Atlanta VFR at low altitude."

There was a silence as he listened. He copied some numbers on the notepad. Then he said, "Terminal forecast for Atlanta and Birmingham?"

More numbers.

"Do you anticipate any early morning ground fog?" He listened, then asked, "Winds, surface and at three thousand?"

He wrote more numbers down. "Thank you," he said. "Piper three oh three six two."

44

As he hung up the phone, Birch said, "Who were you talking to?"

Her grandfather jumped as if he had been shot. "What are you doing up? I thought you went to bed."

"I did, but I came downstairs. I wanted to try one more time to talk you into going to California, but I guess I don't need to do any persuading. Who were you talking to on the phone?"

"That's not any of your business."

"I think it is."

"Birch, go to bed." A frown grew on his face. "And don't wake up your mother. I have had all of her and her garage sale I can take."

"You were talking to flight service about weather, weren't you?"

He glared at the table.

"I know you were because I've heard you talk to them before. And I know why you were talking to them. Because you're getting ready to take off for the coast, aren't you?" With two steps she closed the distance between them.

"I was talking to flight service," he said in a reasonable voice, "because I intend to fly locally tomorrow."

"Huh! It didn't sound local to me—Atlanta—Birmingham. I wouldn't call those local."

She slipped into the chair across from him. He avoided her eyes by putting one freckled hand to his forehead.

"You really are going, aren't you, Pop?"

He leaned back in his chair. He shifted his notepad on the table.

"Answer me."

"I'm going to try it," he admitted.

"Take me."

"Birch, you've just flown in the J-3 for twenty or thirty minutes. It'll be at least thirty hours of flying to the coast, maybe forty, and a lot of waiting around airports—I may be sleeping on the ground."

"I can sleep on the ground. I did it at camp."

"It's going to be noisy. The J-3—"

"Noise doesn't bother me at all. I've been to rock concerts."

"And uncomfortable—the air was smooth today— it's not always going to be like that."

She had her answer ready. "I like uncomfortable air."

"And the main reason, Birch, is that your mother would never forgive me."

"She would."

He shook his head. "She's not going to like it that I'm going, but if I took you—no, she would never forgive me. Closing up the house has made her . . . irrational."

"I could explain it to her later. I could make her understand."

"There's nothing to understand."

"Yes, there is. Pop, I'm not going to be able to explain this to you because all my life, I've had a hard time explaining things. But I am telling you that I have to go.

"Now I know you are going to say what adults always say, 'Oh, no, Birch, be reasonable, Birch, you don't *have* to do anything, Birch.' But I do have to do this. I have to, Pop. Just for once in my life, treat me like a person and believe what I'm saying."

Her grandfather looked out the window where the kitchen light lit up the azaleas.

Birch stretched out her hands, reaching for his. "Please, Pop."

He turned his notepad in a slow circle.

"Birch," he said, "what good sense I've got tells me not to do this. No matter what arguments you give me, no matter how many times you say you have to— my good sense tells me no."

"Pop!"

"But . . ."

She waited.

He looked up and studied her face. His eyes were bright blue. She felt as if she were seeing him when he was seventeen years old, looking up at the sky at that yellow airplane pulling a Freedom banner only he could see.

She drew in a breath. She felt as if the whole world was holding its breath along with her.

"But," he went on, "if everybody in this country had used good sense, we wouldn't even have a country to fly across, would we?"

She shook her head.

"So. If you need to go as bad as you say you do, I'll take you."

Birch flung herself across the table and hugged him. The zeal of her kiss knocked off his Pearle Vision aviator glasses.

CHAPTER 7

The Race of Her Life

 BIRCH OPENED her eyes.

Bright sunlight came through the venetian blinds, making stripes on the bedspread. She stretched, yawned, then stiffened as she heard the sounds of the sale in the yard below.

She threw back the cover and sat up.

Birch had spent the night wide-eyed with excitement. Her grandfather's last words, "Soon as you get up, pack your backpack—your mom'll be suspicious if you take a suitcase—just pack a few things and slip it in the truck."

"I will."

"It's not going to make any difference what you and me have on."

"I'll just take a toothbrush if you tell me to."

"We'll have room for more than a toothbrush. Now go on upstairs and get some sleep."

"I'll try." She had slipped upstairs noiselessly and into her twin bed. "Did you tell Pop?" her mom asked, half asleep.

"What?"

Her mom raised up on one elbow. "I don't know! Whatever you went downstairs to tell him!"

"Oh, yes, that. Good night, Mom."

"Good night!"

Birch had stared up at the ceiling. She knew sleep was impossible. She wasn't even going to try to sleep. She would just lie here and think of flying away, of leaving the world behind.

Then, when the darkness began to thin, Birch had fallen into such a deep sleep that she had not even heard her mother get up.

In one movement she jumped out of bed and reached for her clothes.

She knew Pop was up. Pop was an early riser. He was probably downstairs, waiting impatiently, and he hated to wait. Maybe he was already in the truck.

Hopping toward the door, she pulled on her shorts. Her thoughts darkened.

Maybe Pop had gotten tired of waiting. Maybe he had left for the airport. Maybe he was at this moment taxiing toward runway nine, revving up the engine, turning onto the runway, opening the throttle—

"Pop!" It was a cry of anguish.

She buttoned her shirt as she ran down the stairs. "Pop!"

There was no one in the kitchen. She crossed the hall quickly and looked in his bedroom. The room was empty, the bed unmade.

"Mom!" she wailed. "Pop's gone!"

She ran for the basement stairs. Halfway down, she paused. The basement was packed with people looking over the tables, making selections.

"Oh, look at this. I haven't seen one of these in years. I'm going to get this for . . ."

"I love these old-timey kid gloves. I wish they were bigger. Ladies used to have such tiny hands . . ."

"Mom!"

"Does Bertie have an ice cream maker, do you know? I'd get this for her if . . ."

"I'm in the garage," her mother called cheerfully.

Birch elbowed her way through the people and into the garage where there were more tables, more people.

"Where is Pop?"

"At the airport," her mother said. "Birch, it is going so well. You would not believe how much money I've already made." She flipped open the cigar box so Birch could see the pile of bills.

"Mom, I was going to the airport with him."

"He left early. He had some things to do. He said he'd be back for you."

"You should have called me!"

Her mother turned to speak to a customer. "No,

we're not selling the Christmas lights. Those go with the house . . . The sheet music is ten cents a copy, and the records are twenty-five. The albums—Birch, I'm busy."

"Did he say when he'd be back?"

"I don't remember. Birch, do something with Ace. Everybody's stepping on him. . . . Yes, the toaster works," she told a woman. "All the appliances work."

"Would you take five dollars for the toaster?"

"Not this early in the day, I—"

"Mom!"

"Birch, if you want to make yourself useful, do something with Ace."

"I can't right now. I'll be back."

Birch ran up the stairs, two at a time. She grabbed her backpack and packed in a rush, muttering to herself, "Shirts, shorts . . . What else? Jeans, underwear—Where's my sweatshirt?" She paused in thought. "Oh, toothbrush, toothpaste, comb."

She glanced around the room and her eyes fell on the box of poems. She hesitated because these were what she wanted to leave behind. Something in that box, some unwanted knowledge was the reason she was going.

She crossed the room and stood looking down at the box. She picked it up and poems exploded onto the bed. It was as if they had been waiting for years to get out and would never allow themselves to be shut away again.

She bent, picked up the sheets and laid them back

in the box. Then she put the box in her backpack and zipped it up.

She ran down to the garage.

"Sit by the cash box, will you, Birch?" her mom asked.

"But only until Pop comes. Then I've got to go."

Birch sat at the card table and stuffed her backpack behind her legs. She drummed her fingers impatiently on the cigar box. Her eyes watched the driveway.

Long minutes dragged by. Eight-thirty came. Nine o'clock. Birch's fear began to grow.

Her mom came into view and Birch asked again, "Mom, please try to remember when Pop said he'd be back."

Her mother was talking to one of her friends. "Joyce, I don't know whether all the pieces are there or not." She shook some boxes of jigsaw puzzles and listened to them rattle. "They probably are because Mother was so particular about her puzzles. She finished her last one the day before she died. It was the Mona Lisa. I don't have the heart to sell that one. Oh, listen, just take the puzzles."

"I couldn't. Why, there must be thirty—van Gogh's 'Sunflowers.' Degas's 'Dancing Class.' Your mother must have loved art."

"She did. At one time she painted, or thought about painting. Then she gave it up and just did puzzles of paintings. It's sort of sad when you think about it. Here, take them. She'd want you to have them."

Birch was almost sick with tension. "Mom, I have got to get to the airport."

"Your grandfather said he'd be back for you."

"I've got to go now."

"I'm going by the airport on my way to the island, Liz," Joyce said. "I can drop her off."

Her mother hesitated, and Birch said impatiently, "Please, Mom."

"All right, but if your grandfather isn't there—and he's liable to be on his way home to pick you up—if he isn't there, go in the executive terminal and wait."

"All right."

"And take Ace, Birch. He's starting to growl at people."

"Ace?" Birch paused at the garage door. "I can't take him. He'd be in the way."

"You won't mind if he rides in your car, will you, Joyce? He can sit on Birch's lap."

"Not at all."

"Then it's settled."

Birch picked Ace up and put him under her arm. "You are going to ruin everything," she told him on the way to the car. His tail thumped happily against her back.

Birch slid into the front seat and waited for Joyce to start the car. Joyce was looking out the car window.

"Oh, I hate to see that house sold. I grew up with your mom and we had so many good times there."

"Mom'll miss it too," Birch said.

She sighed with impatience as Joyce pulled away

from the house. She glanced at the speedometer. Thirty-five. They were only going thirty-five! It was the race of her life and they were going thirty-five!

"Picnics on the back lawn, spend-the-night parties. One Halloween we slept up in the attic and your grandfather came up the steps rattling tire chains. We screamed so loud your grandmother said, 'Mr. Earl, go to your room!' "

They stopped for a light. Birch checked her watch. She began to smooth Ace's coarse fur.

"And at Christmas your grandfather put up more lights than anybody, you could see the glow for miles. It was like fireworks."

At last, they pulled into the airport. Joyce said, "I'll wait to make sure your grandfather's here."

"Never mind. I see his truck."

Birch had the door open even before the car came to a halt. A voice said, "Right door is open."

"Oh, sorry," Birch said. She laughed nervously. "Now, I'm apologizing to a car. Anyway, thanks for the ride."

Birch put Ace on the ground and started for the T hangar. "I'll help you attack his shoes this time," she said.

Ace caught up with her at the corner of the hangar and they rounded the building together.

Birch stopped. For a moment she could not believe her eyes. Her mouth dropped open. "Oh, no!" she said.

The hangar doors were open. The hangar was empty. The J-3 Cub was gone.

CHAPTER 8

Empty Hangar, Empty Dreams

"HE'S LEFT ME, ACE. He's gone."

She put one hand over her chest. "I can't bear it, Ace. I just can't bear it."

She slumped to the bench.

Ace walked around the bench and stood at her feet. He waited, his tail slowly sagging between his short hind legs.

"Up until yesterday, Ace, I was a happy person. I was average, but I was happy. And then, I read this poem and it was like a dark cloud came over my life. I wasn't happy anymore. I felt like I might never be happy again. That probably sounds silly to you, but it was one of the strongest feelings I've ever had in my life.

"And then, Ace, Pop agreed to let me fly away with him, across the whole country, and it was like I'd gotten a stay of execution or something. I felt so relieved and, well, almost happy."

She blinked her tears away. "And now, well, I'm more miserable than ever."

Ace's tail gave one tentative wag.

"Don't wag your tail. It's not appropriate. I had this dream last night. I can't remember all of it, but it was about a baby that somehow died . . ."

She slumped forward, not looking at the dog now.

"And in some way, I was responsible . . . It doesn't make sense and yet it would make sense if I knew what I was supposed to know."

She sat without moving. Ace waited and then gave a moan of impatience. She looked up.

"Oh, all right. We better go to the terminal."

She slung her backpack to her shoulder and, kicking a rock ahead of her, she began walking.

"Come on, Ace," she told the dog.

Ace had paused to scratch behind his left ear. Then he trotted after her. At the terminal, Birch held the door open for him.

"Well, I have been abandoned," she told the girl at the counter.

"Oh?"

"I was going on this wonderful trip with my grandfather—to California, and he left without me."

"Who is your grandfather?"

"Earl Bingham. We were going in his J-3 Cub."

57

"Oh, Mr. Earl wouldn't abandon you. I know him. He's a real fine gentleman."

"Then where could he be?"

"Well, he was in here about a half hour ago and bought some new maps. Did you check the hangar?"

"It's empty."

"I mean the maintenance hangar next door. Right through there."

"No, I didn't."

Birch crossed to the door and reached for the knob. Then she stopped.

She didn't want to open the door if he wasn't going to be there. This was her last chance.

"Is it locked?" the girl at the desk asked.

"No."

"Go on in then. It's all right."

Birch took a deep breath. She closed her eyes, reached for the knob and pulled the door toward her.

She opened her eyes, and it was like something out of *The Wizard of Oz.* It was the moment when the black and white world suddenly turns to technicolor.

There was the bright yellow J-3. There was her grandfather in an orange flight suit. Even the sunshine slanting in the hangar door was brighter than regular sunshine. The sky beyond was crayon blue.

Birch ran through the door. Her grandfather turned and she threw her arms around his waist. At their feet, Ace caught the excitement and began to bark.

"Where'd you two come from?" he asked.

"I thought you were gone! Pop, I thought you'd left me!"

"You know I wouldn't do a thing like that."

"But the hangar was empty and—I don't know—I thought you'd gone. I didn't think I could bear it."

"We were changing the oil, that's all. Then I was coming for you. Now that you're already here, we'll take off in ten minutes." He looked at his watch. "A little bit behind schedule, but not much."

"Where do I put my things?"

"That's the luggage compartment." Pop pointed behind the rear seat.

"I am so excited," Birch said. She leaned in the window and stowed her backpack in the compartment. "I've got goose bumps, look. And I hardly brought a thing—one pair of jeans, two pairs of shorts, a box of—some stuff . . ."

"Did you say anything to your mother?"

"Oh, no. I didn't dare. Anyway, she was so involved with the garage sale, I could have gone, 'Mom, I'm leaving now. I'm flying to California,' and she would have said, 'Fine.' "

"I left her a note."

"Pop, she might find it before we get going! She might try to stop us."

"Not with that sale going on. Your mom is very wrapped up in that sale."

"I know, but—"

"I figure she'll find the note about suppertime. We'll give her a chance to read it and cool down.

Then we'll telephone and let her know we're all right."

"But we can't tell her where we are, Pop. She'll come after me. I know she will. She'll drag me home. She won't be able to make you come home, but she'll—"

"We have to call her, Birch. It's—" Pop broke off as the realization hit him that Ace was with her. He looked down. Birch read his thoughts.

"I had to bring Ace, Pop. Mom wouldn't let me come without him."

"Birch—"

"What was I supposed to say? 'I can't take him because we're flying to California?' "

"Birch—"

"I'll hold him on my lap. And, Pop, you know how he hates to be left behind."

"Birch, I wouldn't have left Ace behind. He's the best friend I've got. If you hadn't brought him, I'd have gone back after him. Hey, Ace, you been wanting to go to California bad as me, haven't you, boy?" He picked Ace up. "We—"

The mechanic interrupted. "Anything else, Mr. Bingham?"

"No, thank you for your help."

"You and your granddaughter must be going on a trip."

"That's right. Birch, help me push the plane out of the hangar."

Birch put her hands on the strut. Ace trotted at her heels.

"It's a nice day for flying," the mechanic said. "How far you going?"

Her grandfather looked over his shoulder, and as he said the word a chill of excitement came over Birch.

"California."

"You're going all the way to California in the Cub?"

"That's right."

"Well, you have a nice trip, you hear?"

"We will," Birch called over her shoulder. "We really will!"

CHAPTER 9

Heading: West

 THE J-3 WAS on the run-up area, engine idling. Birch was in the front seat. Her seat belt was tight; her throat was dry.

Pop was in the backseat, and Ace was on the luggage rack behind him. Ace was leaning forward, panting with heat and excitement. Drops of saliva dotted the shoulder of Pop's orange jump suit.

"What are we waiting for, Pop?"

"Talk into the hole," her grandfather said.

Just before they had gotten in the plane, Pop had given her some earphones. "What do we need these for?" she'd asked.

"So we don't have to be yelling all the time. Put them on."

Birch had slipped them over her head and settled them on her ears.

"Now see this tube? That goes right in front of your mouth, and when you've got something to say, you talk into that hole."

Birch asked her question again—this time into the tube. "What are we waiting for?" She felt she would not be able to relax until they were in the air.

"That's better. A Cessna's on final," he told her. "We'll take off after he lands."

Birch squinted at the sky until she saw the airplane. She watched it touch down, roll to the taxiway, and turn off. She looked back at her grandfather and gave the thumbs-up signal.

Pop said, "Ready?"

"I sure am!" She felt as if she had been ready for this all her life, instead of just for one day. "Let's go!"

Pop closed the window and secured it. "Charleston Executive Traffic," he said—Birch could hear his radio transmission in her earphones—"Piper three oh three six two departing runway nine, will be a left downwind departure, westbound."

Westbound—the word itself thrilled her. She took a deep, unsteady breath.

Pop turned onto the runway and pushed the throttle forward. The J-3 started down the runway, picking up speed. It lifted easily into the air.

"Want to fly over the house?" he asked. "Say good-bye?"

63

She shook her head.

"Why not?"

"I don't want Mom to see us."

"She won't."

Her grandfather banked the J-3 and turned north. Birch leaned against the window, watching for landmarks—the steeple of the Episcopal church, the high school, the track, the Bi-Lo parking lot . . .

"There's your house, Pop! I'm glad we did this. There's the tree I was named for—it's the first time I've seen it from the air and—oh, look! Somebody bought the picnic table. They're putting it in a station wagon."

She felt so removed from the house that she could look at it without regret.

Her grandfather circled the block.

"Bye, Mom," Birch said. She put one hand against the window.

She looked over her shoulder at her grandfather. She said, "I guess I ought to feel guilty about doing this, but I don't. I feel wonderful."

"I feel guilty enough for both of us."

Birch took a deep breath of air. She had that freedom her grandfather talked about yesterday. She understood why cowboys yelled and threw their hats in the air, why people tore down goalposts.

Poetry said it all. "My heart leaps up . . ." "I am the captain of my soul . . ." "Up soared the lark into the air . . ."

Heading: West

The lark's on the wing;
The snail's on the thorn;
God's in his Heaven—
All's right with the world.

Well, everything might not be all right with her world, but that wasn't going to catch up with her for a long time. She felt free and alive and—normal again. She was amazed at how good normal felt.

"Take the stick a minute," her grandfather said.

"What?"

"Take the control stick."

"What—wait, I'm not ready. I was in the middle of a poem."

"Hold the stick while I fold my map."

"Pop, wait. I don't know which way to go. I—"

"Hold it like it is." She could hear the impatience in her grandfather's voice through the earphones.

"All right, but I am not ready for this!"

She grasped the control stick uneasily in both hands. Now her throat was dry for a new reason. First from excitement . . . now from nervousness.

"I'm not good at climbing! I told you that yesterday! I can't see! I don't know where I'm going!" Panic made her voice shake. It was as if she were alone in the plane. She strained forward, but all she could see over the cowling was the sky. "I have to see the horizon or something. I—"

"Hold it steady."

"I'm trying! Pop!"

"All right," her grandfather snapped. "I've got it!"

Birch sank back against the seat. She rested for a moment with her eyes closed. Her heart pounded.

In a voice that shook, she said, "I'm sorry if you're irritated with me, but just because I flew for fifteen minutes yesterday, that doesn't mean I'm a professional pilot."

In her earphones, her grandfather's voice said cheerfully, "I can't hear if you're talking to me. Well, say good-bye to the Atlantic Ocean."

Birch glanced over the side of the cockpit at the beach they were leaving behind. A few white clouds had begun to form over the ocean.

"The next ocean you see will be the Pacific."

"Good-bye, Atlantic," she murmured.

Her grandfather turned the J-3 west. Birch watched the compass settle on W. They were still climbing. The altimeter read 1200.

"Want to look at the map—see what to watch for?" He reached over her shoulder. His thumbnail pointed to a pencil-thin line on the folded map.

"We'll follow the railroad—this line. See? And this is a tower—that'll be on our left." His thumb shifted to a blue towerlike symbol. "It's a big one—thirteen hundred thirty-four feet. But by that time we'll be at two thousand. We're already at fifteen hundred."

"Can I hold the map?"

"You don't know what the things mean."

"I might if you'd let me look." She tugged the map, but he did not release it.

"Over here's the city of Walterboro," he went on, "it'll be on our right. This double line is the interstate."

"I want to see where we are now."

"We're somewhere in here." He made a small circular motion over a pale green area.

"In other words, you don't know."

"If you'd help me look for checkpoints I would." His voice was irritated again. "I'm looking for Walterboro."

Birch rested her head against the window. Below the land was mostly forest, but this forest was sectioned off into fields, like a crop.

They flew over a field of felled trees, then a field of new green trees. From the ground this forest probably looked like a regular one, she thought, but from the air it had the sharp look of engineered exactness.

"South Carolina is nothing but one big tree farm," she commented.

"That's where we get our paper."

"Oh." She straightened. "So, where's our first stop?"

"Don't tell me you're already wanting to stop. I can take you back, you know."

"No. No!"

"Oh, yonder's the tower." He pointed through the summer haze. "Now, let's start looking for Walterboro."

CHAPTER 10

"Hi, Mom, Guess What?"

 ''WELL, I DON'T GUESS we can put it off any longer,'' Pop said.

Birch and Pop had checked into a Best Western motel and had eaten supper in the restaurant. The waitress had given them some scraps for Ace.

Now Birch was lying on one of the beds with her backpack beside her. Her eyes were closed. The J-3 engine still roared in her head.

"Put off what?"

"Calling your mother."

Birch sat up abruptly.

Pop said, "That was quick."

"Well, I want to get it over with, same as you."

Pop continued to line up the contents of his pockets on the dresser exactly the way he did at home—his keys, knife, calculator, pen, gas receipts, wallet. He was taking his time.

"I'll dial," Birch said. All at once she was so impatient to talk to her mother that her hands trembled.

She reached for the phone, but Pop was there before her. "You don't know the credit card number. I'll dial. Anyway, I want to talk first."

"Why can't I talk first? I'm the daughter."

"Well, I'm the father."

They eyed each other competitively. Neither of them had combed their hair since they climbed out of the J-3 an hour ago, and they both had bangs down to their eyebrows. Their chins jutted forward at the same angle. They looked as if they'd been cut from the same pattern.

"It'll be better if your mother takes the blame out on me," he said, tugging the phone.

Birch didn't let go.

"And there's going to be plenty of blame, don't kid yourself about that," Pop said.

"Oh, all right."

Birch sat back. She crossed her legs and jiggled her foot in the air while her grandfather dialed.

He listened and frowned at the phone. "I must have done something wrong."

Birch snorted with impatience. "Did you dial a nine? It says right there you have to dial a nine first."

Pop redialed. The phone rang, and Pop ran his

hands through his hair, as if to make himself more presentable for the conversation.

"Liz?" he said in a loud voice. "Lizzie, it's your dad."

All Birch could hear after that was her mother's explosion. Her grandfather held the phone a few inches from his ear to protect his hearing.

"Liz—"

He took another outburst.

"Liz, give me a chance to explain—"

Birch made circles in the air with her foot. Her ankle popped. Maybe it was better that he talked first, she thought. Her mother's anger never lasted long. By the time she got the phone, if she ever did, her mother might even be sorry for Birch.

"Forest, Mississippi," her grandfather yelled, as if he were trying to outshout her. "We're in Forest, Mississippi!"

There was another tirade, shorter this time, but no less intense.

"We flew eight hours. That's how we got so far. I just added it up—five hundred sixty-five miles, the most I ever flew in my life . . . well, I am proud of myself . . . I'm not proud of bringing Birch, of course not . . . She's right here. You want to speak to her?"

He held out the phone. "Your turn."

Birch took it. Her mother's first words were, "Why, Birch, why?"

"Why what?"

"This isn't like you, Birch, running off without a word."

"I know, but I was afraid you would stop me. Pop was afraid you'd stop him too."

"Well, I couldn't have stopped him, but—"

"I'm sorry." Birch's voice quivered.

Pop turned abruptly and went into the bathroom. Birch could hear water running as he splashed his face. She noticed that he left the door open so he could follow the conversation.

"Are you all right, Birch?" her mom asked. "Tell me the truth."

"I'm fine."

"I have the feeling something's wrong."

"No, I'm fine. I just wanted to come on this trip. When did you find out?"

"I came up after the garage sale—incidentally we made over twenty-six hundred dollars—I came up-stairs with a cigar box containing twenty-six hundred dollars which was a very scary feeling. I could have been robbed. I was calling Joyce to ask her to drive me to the bank to deposit the money, when I saw the note. I shook it open, read it, and hung up the phone in Joyce's face."

"I knew you'd be mad, Mom, but—"

"Mad! I was shaking like a leaf. I called your father —got him out of an orthodonics banquet to read him the note. Incidentally did you see it?"

"The note? No."

"Here it is, in its entirety. 'By the time you read this,

Birch and I will be on our way to California in the J-3 Cub. We'll call tonight.' Like you'd gone to the corner drugstore."

"What did Dad say?"

"Actually, I am just as furious at your father as I am at you and Pop."

"Why? What did he say?"

"He laughed."

"Laughed?"

"He has always gotten a kick out of your grandfather. I said, 'I fail to see the humor in this.' He said, 'I think it's great.' "

"Dad said great?"

"He said, 'I would have given anything to fly to California in a J-3 Cub when I was Birch's age. My grandfather had a variety store and wouldn't even let me play with the BB guns.' "

"I can't believe he said great. I thought I'd have to go to the office for a talk. I—"

"I said, 'Does this mean that you are not going to help me get her back?' I already had the road atlas out by this time, figuring how far you had gotten. My thumb was on Alabama. It never occurred to me you'd make Mississippi!"

"Dad said no?"

"Your father never says no, you know that. He said if I thought it was the right thing to do, he would get in the car himself and come get you."

"Is he coming?"

The thought was not upsetting to Birch, because on

the long drive home—eight or nine hours, surely—
she would get the courage to say what was on her
mind. She longed to hear her dad say, "You thought
what? Oh, Birch, no. Nothing like that ever happened.
It was just a poem. You know your grandmother. She
was probably afraid something like that would happen, and so she . . ."

Her mother was still talking. "But, he also said that
he wanted me to think about it, because he thought it
could be a wonderful experience, the kind of thing
you would remember all your life."

"Is he coming?"

"So I gave it some thought, and while I do not approve of the way you and Dad did this—I don't like
that one bit. While I do not approve of the way you
did it, I'm not going to stop you."

"You aren't?"

"No."

"Dad's not coming?"

"No. Now, tell me all about it," her mother said,
her tone changing to friendly interest. "Is it exciting?"

"I'm numb, Mom, we flew eight hours."

"At least you had a beautiful day for it."

"Well, I wouldn't say beautiful. It rained in Georgia."

"I don't think I could have stood it if it had rained
here. The thought of a sale in the rain is—" She
broke off. "Your grandfather stops to rest every now
and then, doesn't he? He used to hate to stop when
we went on trips. That's the one thing I remember

about our vacations. Mom and I begging to stop and Dad pretending not to hear us. You do stop sometimes, don't you?"

"We have to stop, Mom, the J-3 only holds twelve gallons of gas. We stopped at Louisville and Warm Springs. They're both in Georgia, and Birmingham, Alabama. Oh, at the Birmingham airport a man had just soloed and they were cutting off his shirttail."

Her grandfather came out of the bathroom, drying his sunburned face on a towel. "Is it safe for me to talk now?"

Her mom said, "Is that Dad?"

"Yes."

"Put him on, Birch. He will flip when he hears what I got for the porch swing. Now, Birch, I want you to promise to call me every single night."

"I will."

Wordlessly, she held out the phone to her grandfather. Pop paused as if reluctant to take it.

"It's all right. She's not going to stop us," Birch said with a sigh. "She wants to tell you about the sale."

Pop threw his towel into the air in celebration. He caught it and did an old timey fox-trot step with it as his partner. Then he draped the towel around his neck and took the telephone.

CHAPTER 11

Bimbo and the Mississippi River

 BIRCH WAS in the front seat of the J-3. She glanced above her at the skylight, at the rectangle of bright, cloudless blue sky windowed there. The front had passed through during the night, and the morning air was crystal clear.

"CAVU," Pop had said.

"What does that mean, Pop?"

"Ceiling and visibility unlimited. You'll probably be able to see for a hundred miles."

They had taken off at 7:40 and were now flying westward over Mississippi.

Birch glanced out the window. Below the broad ribbed wing of the J-3, lay the interstate.

The interstate stretched as far as the eye could see.

It had taken on a special beauty in the clean early morning sunlight—the pale side-by-side ribbons of highway, the scattering of greenery between, the double bridges, the perfectly symmetrical cloverleaf ramps. The rest stops with the parked trucks and cars were as appealing as toys.

Her grandfather touched her shoulder to get her attention.

"You can get an idea of how fast we're going from the traffic. See that Roadway truck?"

She nodded.

"It's probably doing seventy or seventy-five. We've got a little head wind today, so we're probably doing sixty. See how he's moving ahead of us?"

Birch nodded again. She grinned at him over her shoulder.

Pop had told her that morning at breakfast that things would be easier today. "We won't have to be doing any navigating. We'll just follow the interstate. And there won't be a cloud in the sky."

"I got tired yesterday."

"I did myself."

"And I was nervous at times. You probably didn't notice."

"I noticed."

"I had to come on this trip. I had to."

"I did myself."

"But not like me."

He looked at her for a moment, squinting as if to get a better perspective.

She went on quickly. "Anyway, I knew when I woke up this morning that it was going to be a good day. You know how I knew?"

"How's that?"

"Because on the TV news was a story about Bimbo the goat. Didn't you see it?"

"Nope."

"First I have to explain that what I see on the news affects my whole day, like if there's a disaster, I think about those people for the rest of the day. And today, I especially needed to feel good, and when I saw this goat—his name was Bimbo—I knew I would.

"This goat started dancing after his kids were born. His dancing was—well, some people would call it jumping up and down—but it was in time to the music. The music was 'Celebrations.' "

"I only saw the weather."

"Well, he had a lot of rhythm for a goat."

Birch looked out the window. The early morning air was calm and the J-3 rode smoothly.

She was taking more interest in the landscape now that she understood her map. There was real satisfaction in seeing that every curve in the road was on the map, every river. She could find each town and call it by name. Her thumb, like Pop's, was on the exact spot on the map where they were right now.

She noticed on the map that the railroad tracks moved away from the interstate. She looked ahead, and the real railroad tracks slanted away from the highway too.

Birch watched a slow-moving freight train coming toward them. It seemed so toylike, so appealingly slow, that she understood how people got the idea of jumping on board. It was the kind of spur-of-the-moment thing she and Pop might have done if they'd lived near the tracks instead of the airport. He would go, "All my life, I've dreamed of hopping a train to California," and she'd go, "What's stopping us?"

"See that fire over there?" Pop pointed to some columns of smoke on the horizon.

Birch nodded.

"You can tell by the direction of the smoke that the wind's out of the west."

"It looks like a forest fire."

"Brush fire, probably."

There were ugly stripped forests here too, but a row of tall trees had been left by the interstate so travelers would have a good impression of Mississippi.

"Oh, there's another plane, Pop, and—I ain't believing this—it's lower than we are."

Pop said, "Crop duster."

Birch watched the red and white plane skimming the trees below.

"You want to fly some?" Pop asked.

"Sure."

Birch took the control stick in her right hand. She looked at the altimeter. "You want me to stay at three?"

"That'll be fine."

"Pop, I'm really catching on to this. Did you notice how cool that sounded. Shall I stay at three?"

Pop reached around and took Ace from the luggage rack. He put him on his lap. "Good dog," he said, "you didn't know you were going to California, did—"

"Pop, watch me now."

"I am."

"Don't play with the dog."

"I thought you were so cool."

"Pop, I just put my hand on the stick! I haven't had a chance to mess up!"

"I'm watching."

Birch glanced out the window to make sure she hadn't gotten too far from the interstate, then back at the altimeter. "Oh." She pushed forward gently on the stick. When the needle pointed just below three thousand feet, she leveled off. "It went up by itself."

Pop said, "My flight instructor used to say, 'Head up and out, son.' "

"Up and out?"

"What he meant was not to stare at the instruments. Give a quick glance at the instruments, then at the attitude of the plane's nose, the wingtip position, then a three hundred sixty-degree check for traffic. Then back at the—oh, there's Vicksburg and the Mississippi!"

Birch leaned forward and looked over the cowling. "That is the Mississippi River?"

"Yes."

"Pop, I'm disappointed. I expected it to be this

great, wide, rolling river. It looks gray. And when I think of all the songs that have been written about it."

"If you think the Mississippi's a disappointment," Pop said, "wait till you see the Rio Grande. This time of year you can step across it."

Birch felt a sharp move of the stick, and the J-3 turned left. Startled, she said, "Pop, did you do that?"

"Yes."

"Well, tell me when you're going to take over. Don't just grab the stick. It makes me think something's wrong when the stick jerks like—"

"I want to get a picture of you with the river in the background. Look over your shoulder, Birch."

Birch glanced over her shoulder and Pop took a picture of her and the Mississippi River.

"Watch your altitude."

"Well, make up your mind. I can't watch my altitude and pose for a picture at the same time." She pushed forward on the stick.

"You're doing fine, isn't she, Ace? She's doing just fine."

"Well, I am doing better," she admitted.

CHAPTER 12

Texas at Three O'clock

"YOU KNOW WHAT INSTRUMENTS I don't understand?"

"Which ones?" Pop asked. He was on a ladder, putting gas in the plane. They were at the Lancaster County airport, south of Dallas.

This was their third stop of the day. Birch was keeping a list of all the airports they stopped at. Rayville, Louisiana, Marshall, Texas, and now Lancaster.

"I understand the compass—well, let's say I've learned to live with the compass, and I understand the altimeter—it tells height, and—"

"Height above sea level, not above the ground," Pop said.

"I said I understood!" Birch was sitting on a bench,

sharing a pack of cheese crackers with Ace. A thin collie watched intently from the gas pumps.

Birch threw half a cracker to Ace. "I understand oil pressure and oil temperature—that's like a car."

"So what don't you understand?"

"I'm getting to that. The air speed indicator."

"That's like the speedometer in a car."

"Yes, but it always reads sixty-five or seventy when really we could be going forty-five miles an hour or ninety."

"It gives you your speed through the air."

"Which actually means nothing. I also don't see the purpose of the tachometer."

"The tachometer tells you how fast your engine is running, so you don't overtax the engine or use too much gas." Pop wiped his hands on a paper towel. "You ready to stop for the day or you want to keep going?"

"What time is it?"

"Three o'clock. We picked up an hour."

"Oh, let's keep going. I like flying over Texas. Everything's so open. I liked the Blacklands." She said the word dramatically.

"My granddaddy worked there for a while."

"In the Blacklands?"

"He drilled salt wells. Then he met my grandmama. My grandmama was the most superstitious woman ever born. At night she'd turn her pockets inside out to ward off ghosts. If you had a wart, she'd steal a dishrag and hide it, and the wart would go away."

"I never thought of you as having grandparents," Birch said.

He eyed her for a moment. "Believe it or not, I am human."

"I didn't mean that. I never thought of you with grandparents who moved around," she added.

"Why's that?"

"Because you stayed in one place your whole life. You worked at one job."

"Maybe I liked my job. Did you ever think of that?"

"You liked maintaining machines?"

He ducked under the wing.

"I didn't mean that as an insult."

"I didn't take it as one. Yes, I liked maintaining machines. Well, let me pay for my gas and check out a J-3 they're restoring in the hangar. Then we'll get going."

"I'm beginning to think every airport in the United States has two things—a J-3 being restored in the hangar and a dog."

"You want to see the J-3?"

"No, I'm enjoying the Texas sun." She stretched out her legs as Pop wheeled away.

Ace had given up on getting any more crackers and gone to check out the collie. The two dogs were now circling each other warily by the gas pumps.

"Be friendly now," Birch called.

A man came out of the terminal. "Where you folks going in the J-3?" he asked.

"California."

He looked interested. "Where are you planning to cross the San Gabriel Mountains?"

Birch had not been aware there would be mountains. She said, "I don't know. Where do most people cross?"

"Banning's about the lowest. I hope for your sake the winds aren't blowing from the west."

"Why? Because we'd be slow?"

"Because you could get pushed into the ground. I'm a flat-country boy myself. At Banning's where I learned about downdrafts."

Birch sat up straighter. "What are downdrafts?"

"The wind is pushed up one side of the mountain and then when it goes over the top, it starts down and it'll be chopped up and rough. You come to this down slope side and you sink, sometimes below the mountaintop and—"

Her grandfather came around the terminal building then, combing his hair with his hands.

"Pop, I'm talking to this man about going over the mountains."

Pop asked, "Which mountains?"

She turned to the man. "What was the name of those mountains? I don't even know which mountains we're going to be pushed into."

"We're not getting pushed into any mountain," Pop said.

"I was talking about the San Gabriels," the man said. "I had a bad experience at Banning last year—"

He broke off and watched the J-3 Cub. "Well, look at that."

"What?" Birch turned and looked too.

As they watched, the right front tire slowly went flat and the right wing tilted down. Pop said, "Oh," as if the air had gone out of him at the same time.

In the silence that followed Birch said, "What are you going to do, Pop? Do you have a spare?"

He shook his head.

"Can you get one?" Birch got to her feet.

"Not likely."

Birch looked at her grandfather, the downward slope of his shoulders. "Whoopee!"

He looked at her sharply.

"What was that for?"

"Now I get to see you do your thing." She grinned. "Maintain machines." She pushed her sun visor back on her head and challenged him with her eyes.

Pop ground his teeth and turned to the man, "Will you help me get the tire off and see the damage?"

"I'll be glad to."

"I guess the first thing to do is get the weight off of it."

"I'll get some blocks. Buck, give us a hand here," the man called to the line boy.

Birch watched while the men lifted the J-3 wing and put wooden blocks under the axle. Then Pop came to life. In five minutes he had the hubcap off, the cotter key out, and the nut and wheel off.

With the wheel in his hand, Pop started for the

hangar. He said to Birch, "I got to take the tire off and check the inner tube. There's a man here who might be able to fix it. If not, we'll have to take it into town. And this is a new inner tube too. I paid eighty dollars for it."

Birch followed. "Pop, can I ask one more thing about the mountains?"

"You let me worry about the mountains."

"Well, it would be me getting pushed into them too, you know."

"Nobody's going to get pushed into any mountains. Right now we got one thing to worry about and one thing only—this here tire." He shook the wheel at her. "When we get to California—and it looks more like *if* we get to California, then we'll worry about the San Gabriel Mountains."

Birch walked slowly back to the bench and sat down. Ace and the airport collie had finished smelling each other and lost interest. The collie was lying in the shade.

Birch felt the heat as an actual force. Her shoulders sagged.

"Ace, you know what?"

Ace's tail brushed the dry ground.

"Last night, Ace, I had bad dreams again. It didn't have anything to do with flying. It had to do with something in my past.

"This baby had died," she went on, looking down at her hands, "and it must have been my mom's because the doctor was talking to her. He said, 'Don't bother about it. Just take this other one.' And my mom was crying. She didn't want me—I was the other one. She wanted the dead baby. 'Give me my baby,' she kept saying.

"And it was so real, it was like it had actually happened, like I heard those exact words, and even though I heard them when I was a baby, they went into my brain and got stored and . . ."

Birch trailed off. She looked down into Ace's sympathetic eyes.

"It doesn't sound like such a bad dream, I guess. But when I woke up, I was all sweaty and there were tears on my cheeks.

"And I wanted to wake Pop up, right then, in the middle of the night, because I know he could explain that dream.

"As soon as I get a chance, Ace, I'm going to ask Pop to do just that."

CHAPTER 13

Double Exposure

''O NE TIME WHEN I was little—I know you must be getting bored hearing about when I was little, Pop, but there's nothing else to talk about. Also, little things that happened back then keep popping into my mind.''

Birch's words were muffled by the steady drone of the engine.

"Anyway, I was about four or five when this happened. We had been to Myrtle Beach, and my dad had taken lots of pictures of me.

"And one of the pictures was a sort of double exposure. There were two of me, in side by side inner tubes. I said, 'Oh, I'm twins!'

"Well, my mom pulled the picture out of my hand

and tore it up. She didn't even look at it. And I said, 'I wanted that picture! That was my favorite picture!' And my mom went out of the room.

"My dad said, 'Want me to show you my favorite?' And he started turning through the pictures, but as if his mind was on something else—my mom, probably. I felt an undercurrent—something going on that I couldn't see, like they were always warning me about when I went in the ocean, and—"

"What are you muttering about up there?" Pop asked.

"Nothing."

"Well, I can't hear you unless you talk into the tube."

"I know. I was just remembering something that happened. Oh, Pop, we're getting low on gas," Birch said.

This was the third day and they had been flying for four hours. First stop: Cisco, Birch had written. Second stop: She was still waiting to fill that in.

"I said we are low on gas."

"Did you see that town back there? That was Eastland," Pop said, "and I knew there was something about Eastland I wanted to remember. I finally thought of it."

"Pop—"

He went on, unhurried. "The people of Eastland buried a horned toad in the courthouse and it stayed buried thirty years and then it got revived. That toad

89

had its picture taken with Calvin Coolidge. I hope no-body revives me after thirty years."

"Don't try to divert me. We're low on gas."

Birch kept watching the gas gauge. The wire was right in front of her face, just beyond the windshield.

When the tank was full, the gas wire stuck up twelve inches into the air. Then, as the gas was used, the cork would sink with the fuel level. When she could only see one inch of wire, she always started to worry.

Birch could now see one inch of wire. She said, "Pop, I'm really getting worried."

There was always something to worry about, she thought. Like yesterday, with the tire. Then when they got the tire fixed, Pop said, "Looks like it's leaking a little gas." Then he spent a half hour fiddling with something called the sump bowl.

But the gas gauge was her special, personalized worry, because it was never out of her sight. "Where are we going to land?"

"Right here," he told her. He pushed his map over her shoulder and pointed with his thumbnail to a magenta dot beside the double line of the highway.

Birch found it on her own map. "It doesn't even have a name," she said. "If an airport doesn't have a name, I know it won't have a cold drink machine."

Pop didn't comment.

"Plus, we may not make it," Birch said. "You said we were only making fifty-six miles an hour."

She slumped in her seat. It was lonely in front by

herself. At first she had liked it. It was like being in the prow of a boat. She was the first to see everything. Now she felt differently.

"Pop, can I ask you something?"

"If it's not about where and when we're going to land and how much gas we're using."

"It's not. Pop, do you ever get lonely?"

He hesitated. "No more than most old people. That's one reason I asked your mother to help me sell the house. I was trying to get away from some of that."

"How about on this trip? In the J-3, like right now?"

"No. You're in front of me and Ace is behind. I couldn't be lonely with good company like that."

"You know when I go on trips with my cousins, I have to sit in the backseat with them and they pass the time, Pop, by dividing up the world. Frances goes, 'This is my street.' Barb goes, 'Well, that's my street over there. I have a mall and all you have is a Pizza Hut.' Frances goes, 'I claim that house with a tower.' Barb goes, 'Well, I claim that one. It's got a swimming pool.' "

"So what do you claim, Birch?"

"Nothing, but it keeps me from getting lonely. If I were going to claim something," she went on firmly, "I'd claim an airport so we could land. I know you don't want me to say anything, *but!*" She pointed to the gauge.

"I got eyes."

There was a little bend on the end of the gas wire, and it turned, periscopelike, from side to side with the engine vibration. It seemed to be looking for a landing spot too.

Pop asked, "Can you see the airport yet?"

She pulled herself erect by the support bars and peered through the windshield. "I think so." She checked the magenta circle on her map. There was a white line in the circle that showed which way the runway lay. The runway ahead lay the same way.

"That's it." Birch took off her earphones and shook out her hair. Without earphones, the noise was terrible.

"My neck's hot. My feet are hot. I'm ready to stop. I just figured out why my feet are so hot. They're on the engine!"

Pop began his descent. He flew over the airport, circled it and then kept heading west.

Birch swirled around. "Aren't we stopping?"

"See those yellow X's on the runway?"

Birch leaned against the window.

"Those X's mean the airport's closed. We'll go on to Big Spring."

"Pop, when we landed at Cisco, you said we had a head wind."

"We've still got it." Pop checked his computer. "We've been flying two hours. We've gone—let's see, one hundred twelve miles. We've got another half hour of flying time. You watch for the airport."

"You always tell me to watch for things to make me shut up."

Birch bent over her map. Her grandfather had marked off the route and put a slash every ten miles. She counted the slashes, "It's thirty miles . . . let's see. If we have a half hour of gas left and we're only making fifty-six miles an hour—Pop, we'll miss it by two miles!"

"You could be right."

"Pop!"

"There's another airport northeast of town. Howard County airport. It's marked closed, but it won't hurt to take a look."

Birch checked her map. The closed airport was big with multiple runways. She sat forward tensely. The gas wire was all the way down and had not bobbed for what seemed like hours.

"This is the third airport in a row that's been closed. Now, where is it? We ought to be able to see it by now. There! There it is!" She pointed. "It's . . ."

She trailed off. Then she said, "Pop, it's got stuff on the runway."

"What kind of stuff?"

"Tires and bales of hay. They've made it into a drag strip or a racetrack or something."

"I don't want to try to cross town with no more gas than we've got. Let me take a look."

Pop circled the airport while Birch clasped her hands beneath her chin. "Please don't let us give out of gas. Please don't let us give out of gas. At least when you're praying in an airplane you're bound to be noticed, don't you think so, Pop? Please don't let us give out of gas."

"We're not going to give out of gas. Now find me some smoke or dust so I know where the wind's coming from."

Birch pointed to a yarnlike wisp of smoke on the horizon.

"Straight out of the west. I'll land on that taxiway."

"Where the tires are?"

"I'll go over the tires and stop before the bales of hay. Don't talk to me for a minute."

He pushed the nose of the plane down and began his descent. The airspeed indicator moved slowly from 75 miles per hour to 85.

Birch pulled her seat belt tighter. Please, please let us make it.

Pop lined up parallel to the taxiway. He pulled on the carburetor heat. He throttled back and slowed to sixty miles per hour. He made a left turn, then another. Now he was on final.

He came in low and slow, as if he had been practicing for this all his life. Then he settled the Cub gently on the taxiway beyond the tires. He stopped well short of the bales of hay.

"Pop! Wonderful!" Birch turned to grin at him. "Wonderful!"

Pop allowed himself to smile before shrugging off her praise. "Now, let's taxi to the hangar and see if we can scare up some gas."

CHAPTER 14

Two Bags Full

''THIS IS WHAT'S KNOWN as high noon out here,'' Birch said.

She and Ace were sitting under the wing of the J-3. Birch's long legs were crossed under her, out of the brutal Texas sun. Ace was panting with the heat.

"There isn't a shade tree within fifty miles."

Birch and Ace were alone.

After Pop had taxied around the bales of hay, across an old runway and through a gate, and stopped in front of the hangar, the three of them had gotten out of the plane. Ace shook himself while Birch and Pop stood in absolute silence. They took in the locked, abandoned hangar, the weeds growing up through the cracked pavement. There was not a person in sight.

"Pop," Birch said.

"Now don't start worrying. Somebody'll turn up."

"But what if they don't?"

Pop turned on his heels and walked off, whistling through his teeth. Birch moved into the shade of the wing, shoulders sagging. She poured a cup of warm water from the thermos and gave some to Ace.

She heard Pop call, "Anybody home?" again and again, but there was never an answer.

He came back shaking his head. "I can't raise anybody." He reached under the seat for the folded gas bags. "I'm going for gas. You stay with the plane."

"By myself?"

"You and Ace."

Birch looked around at the deserted rusty buildings. The old metal doors on the hangar rattled in a dry breeze. "Deserted airports are as creepy as haunted houses," she said.

"We're lucky the J-3 can use car gas. All I have to do is find a filling station."

"Can't I come? I really don't want to be by myself."

"Keep her company, Ace!"

He was at the chain link fence, tossing the gas bags over, climbing. He jumped, landed on the hard dry dirt, picked up the bags and moved on down the road. He was whistling again.

Pop was one of that hard, stringy breed of men who crossed the country in the first place, Birch thought. Men that cut down forests and plowed land and scaled mountains and then looked around for something else to do. "He's not made of flesh, Ace, like you and me. He's pure gristle." And with a sigh, she settled under the wing for a long wait.

Now Birch reached out and scratched Ace behind the ear. The dog rolled his eyes gratefully in her direction. "And you're probably hotter than I am," she said, "because you've got all this black fur." She sighed.

"I really thought we were going to crash, Ace. And when something like that happens to a person, like almost crashing, well, your whole life is supposed to pass in front of your eyes. You know what passed in front of my eyes? A poem that my grandmother wrote.

"It was about a baby that died, Ace, on my birthday. And all of a sudden I knew that poem meant one of two things. Either my mom's natural baby died—or lived just a little while. Five breaths is a very little while. And so maybe—this is probably not what happened exactly, but maybe someone else in the hospital had had a baby and was going to put her up for adoption, and that was me. And my mom and dad adopted me." She trailed off, shaking her head.

"The reason I don't think that happened is because my mom would tell me that right off. 'You are adopted.' But, then, she didn't tell me about being named for a tree right off, so maybe . . ."

Birch recrossed her legs, brushed some gravel off

the sides, and looked again at her watch. "We've been here an hour.

"The other thing—and this really bothers me—the other thing is that the baby that died was—" She couldn't say the word. She backed up. "Everyone is always telling me how big and healthy I was. I weighed nine pounds! And so you have to figure that if I weighed nine pounds, I pretty much used up all the vitamins and all the minerals and whatever else there was. And if there was another baby there—a twin." It was a word she could not keep avoiding. "If there was a twin, there wouldn't be any nourishment for him, or her, because I was hogging it all. It's like I was a murderer almost. I just hate the thought of myself taking and taking and—"

She heard the sound of a truck and got to her feet. Moving into the sunlight, she shaded her eyes and saw Pop climbing out of a pickup truck. He reached back inside for two bags of red gas.

"Meet me at the fence," he called.

"I hope he thought to get me something to drink, Ace."

Pop was lifting the first bag over the fence when she got there. "It's heavy," he warned. She set it down and reached for the second.

He said, "You gas up the plane while I take the truck back."

"Pop, I don't know how to . . ."

He was already in the truck, backing up. He drove away in a column of dust.

Birch lugged the bags of gas to the plane. "Did you hear that, Ace? He goes, 'Gas up the plane.' I'd like to know who he'd have ordered around if I hadn't come."

She reached to the top of the cowl and unscrewed the gas cap. She lifted it off, being careful with the cork-tipped stick. With an, "Oof," she heaved the gas bag onto the cowling.

She turned the cap on the gas bag, and gas began to flow into the airplane. "Next he'll go, 'Change the oil. Fix the flat. Do this. Do that. Fly the airplane. Do a triple loop . . .' "

The gas was almost out of the first bag when her grandfather arrived on foot. Birch watched as he climbed the fence. "Pop, you better get out of the sun. Your face is red."

"It's always red."

"Not this red, Pop."

"Well, I have been all over the county," he said cheerfully. "I walked till I found the caretaker. He lives in a mobile home about a mile down the road. He wanted to help—Texans like to be of help—but he didn't have a car. His aunt's car was up on blocks, so he cut a section out of his garden hose and we tried to siphon out some gas. It was too low. I'll take that."

Birch folded up the empty gas bag while he talked.

"So then I kept going and found somebody with a pickup and got directions to the nearest gas station which was five miles down the road." He emptied the second bag and folded it up. "It took all ten gallons and is still a gallon from full. That figures to be about four gallons an hour for the previous flight—and we had at least a gallon left, so we could have made the seven miles across town."

"Now you tell me."

"Okay, let's go."

"Pop, didn't you even bring me a cold drink?"

"We'll get drinks later."

"That's what you always say. When later? All I've had is a cup of stale water!"

"Be thankful."

Pop pulled the chocks out from the wheels. He took the wing and slowly swung the plane around.

"Get in."

"Pop—"

"If you're going with me, get in."

Birch took her time putting Ace on the luggage rack and getting into the front seat. She buckled her belt, put her heels on the brakes.

"Brakes and contact."

"Brakes. Contact!" He swung the prop and the plane came to life. Birch watched through the whirling blur of the prop as they taxied the way they had come. "Watch the wings," Pop said as they went through the gate.

"I'm watching."

When they were lined up facing the wind, Pop said, "At least this head wind will shorten our takeoff distance. Is your belt tight?"

"My belt stays tight." She looked through the shimmering heat at the line of tires blocking the taxiway. "You're sure we're going to make this?"

"We got two thousand feet. It's a piece of cake."

He slid the throttle forward. Birch closed her eyes and held on tight.

She felt the wheels leave the ground, and she opened her eyes in time to see them lift off halfway to the bales of hay and turn toward the city of Big Spring.

Sighing she leaned back and watched the Texas landscape below without interest. She was tired and hungry and hot. Sweat ran down the backs of her legs. "He could at least have brought me a coke," she muttered.

Neither of them spoke for an hour. Birch sat with her arms crossed over her chest. It was Pop who broke the silence. "That's the Midland–Odessa area ahead."

"Nice airport," she said pointedly. "They probably have a cold drink machine."

"Oil storage tanks down there, but they're empty."

"I'm not that interested in oil storage."

In some fields all that remained of the tanks were the pale circles where they had been. In the distance oil well pumps rocked back and forth on the dry, cactus-dotted landscape.

"The only place trees are of any size is the cemetery," Pop commented.

"Oh, look!" she cried, leaning forward. "A swimathon! Those lucky, lucky people. Pop, I want to be in that pool so bad I'd jump if I had a parachute."

"You want to fly some?" Pop asked.

She closed her eyes. I am hot and tired and sweaty and getting too close to something I don't like. The last thing I want to do in the whole world is fly.

She opened her eyes. She said, "Oh, all right, I'll fly a while," and she took the control stick.

CHAPTER 15

Almost Across Texas

 ''HI, DAD, it's me, checking in.''

"Birch, where are you?"

"Monohans, Texas."

"Wait a minute. Let me open your mom's map. Hey, you're almost across Texas."

"Almost."

"So what did you do today?"

"We did what we always do—we flew and flew and flew."

"I'd like to hear some details."

"Well, we flew three hundred eighty miles—Pop just figured it out. We had a head wind. It took us six hours and twenty-eight minutes. We used twenty-six and one tenth gallons of gas."

"Where'd you land?"

"First we landed at Cisco. There was nobody there. There wasn't even a drink machine. Dad, a lot of Texas airports are deserted, but a real nice man in a Honda took Pop to the gas station. I waited with his wife. She told me she joined the Civil Air Patrol so she could fly and she marched for three years.

"Then we gassed up and went on to the next airport which had been turned into a race—"

She hesitated, because her grandfather gave her a warning look.

"We landed on an airport which is not used much anymore—for airplanes."

Pop allowed himself to smile.

"So once again Pop went for gas and I waited. I was so hot I was panting harder than Ace. Then we put the gas in and flew to Monohans, and I was so happy to be here I fell down and kissed the ground like the Pope. We're at the Holiday Inn, getting ready to go to the seafood buffet. Where's Mom?"

"She's over at Joyce's."

"Oh. And, Dad, guess what? I saw my first mesa today. The west looks just like it's supposed to look."

"Are you doing any of the flying?"

"I fly all the time. It's like driving. I stay on the right side of the interstate and maintain my altitude. I can tell how fast I'm going by the traffic. Today we went slow. The only vehicle we passed was a motor home."

"How's Ace?"

"Ace's doing fine. He gets out of the plane when we

land, finds a weed to go to the bathroom on and then he's ready to get back in. He went on a cactus today—that was another first."

There was a pause, and her dad said, "Actually, I'm glad your mom's not here at the moment."

"Oh?" Birch felt a pang of unease.

"Yes, I want to talk to you."

"Oh?"

"Birch, I'm sure you are aware that your mom's been under a lot of pressure lately."

"Yes."

"That's one of the reasons I came down. Selling the house and going through all those memories has been hard on her."

"I was there, remember?"

"Yes. In some ways, Birch, your mom got out of touch with what was going on around her. And now that she's getting more in control, she's starting to wonder about things."

"Like what?"

"Like that box of your grandmother's poems, for one thing."

"Oh."

"She looked for it after you left. She wanted to check one of the poems, but the box was missing."

"I brought it with me."

"She was particularly concerned, Birch, about the poem written on your birthday."

"I was concerned about that too."

"It's something we need to talk about."

"Yes, but not over the phone—please."

"No, not over the phone."

She was surprised that she felt relief.

"As soon as you get back—"

"I'll come down to the office," she finished for him, forcing a laugh. Then she said, "Oh, here's Pop. He wants to say something."

Birch handed the phone to Pop and went into the bathroom. She drank a glass of water and watched herself in the mirror. The talk with her dad had made her tense and now, as she relaxed, her knees began to tremble.

She closed her eyes against her reflection. She was still standing there, leaning against the basin, eyes closed when Pop called, "You ready to eat?"

"Yes, I'm starved!"

She joined him, and they walked out into the late afternoon heat. It was five o'clock and the sky was building with towering cumulous clouds. Birch heard a rumble of thunder in the distance.

"We'll have thunderstorms tonight."

"Just so we don't have them when we're flying. Have you ever flown in a thunderstorm, Pop?"

"Not since the war."

Birch pushed open the door to the dining room. "Oh, look, Pop. We're the first ones. I love to be first at a buffet. We're not too early, are we?" she asked the waitress.

"No, help yourself."

"This looks so good. I'm going to start with fruit."

She filled a plate with cantaloupe, honey dew melon, pineapple, salad, strawberries.

She sat down opposite her grandfather and put a strawberry in her mouth. "This is the best strawberry I ever ate in my life. One bad thing about a life of starvation is that when you finally get food—you make a pig out of yourself!"

She stopped talking. She put the half-eaten strawberry down on her plate and looked at it. "Is there such a thing as being too hungry to eat?"

"Not for me."

Birch picked up the half-eaten strawberry and looked up. "Oh, I know what I wanted to ask you. Will you tell me the truth?"

"I'm too tired to lie."

"Were we in danger today when we landed on the drag race track? I wasn't nearly as scared as I thought I would be."

"No, that was an old military airport. The taxi strip was as wide as most runways. I did a lot of landings in the war that made that one look like a piece of cake. I'm not going to take any risks. This trip is important to me."

"Well, it's important to me too, but—" She shrugged.

"But it's not your last chance."

"Pop, don't say things like that."

"When your grandmother lay dying—"

"Oh, Pop, please don't."

"When your grandmother lay dying, she didn't

know what she was saying half the time, or maybe she did. But she talked about the things she hadn't done."

"Like what?"

"It turned out she'd always wanted to go to England. She'd never said a word about that to me. She wanted to visit the homes of poets. She could call out the names of their houses. She wanted to write books and paint pictures. Come to find out she never did care much for all those puzzles I bought her and she made such a fuss over."

"She loved doing those puzzles."

"Well, you wouldn't have known it to hear her at the end."

"Pop, at the end she was on so much pain medicine she didn't know what she was saying."

"But on her deathbed, she had regrets." He took a breath. "When I lay dying—"

"Pop, now stop it! I mean it! I'm putting my fingers in my ears!"

"When I lay dying, if I babble—and most people do —I want to babble about landing on a racetrack at Big Spring, about coming through the Soledad pass and seeing the Pacific, about taking off at dawn at Monohans, Texas, about—"

"Dawn, Pop? Why does it always have to be dawn?" Birch dropped her hands into her lap. "Just once couldn't we take off at ten o'clock in the morning?"

CHAPTER 16

Dawn Patrol

 POP WAS CHECKING under the cowling. "This thing was trying to leak a little bit the other day."

Birch slumped beside Ace. "I thought that was the sump bowl."

A small crayon-streak of peach was on the horizon. A red, half-circle of sun moved into sight.

"I have seen more sunrises . . ." Birch trailed off without finishing her sentence.

The three of them had fallen into a morning routine. Birch awoke as soon as Pop pulled aside the motel drape to check the colorless, predawn sky. He would be already dressed in his jumpsuit. Ace would be at the door, waiting to go for his walk.

"What time is it?" she'd ask, squinting at them.

"Five-thirty."

"Pop! Why so early?"

"It's seven-thirty our time."

While Birch struggled out of bed and into her clothes, Pop walked Ace and looked for a ride to the airport. They'd drive through empty streets. Dawn was Pop's favorite time of day. "There's an air of reason and peace about it. I feel like I'm getting a jump on the rest of the world," he'd say.

"I'm not a morning person," Birch would answer.

The airport would be deserted too. As the sun came up, Birch would be undoing the ropes that held the wings and Pop would be checking the plane.

Now Pop secured the cowling. "I'm setting the altimeter on twenty-six thirteen, see? That's the elevation of the field. Did you notice that your map looks browner than it did back in South Carolina?"

"Not really."

"The green color on a sectional stands for low land. As the land gets higher . . . Open up your map."

She pulled out her map and unfolded it. "See the background color is brown? And when we get beyond Pecos, see, it gets even browner. Here are the three thousand-foot contour lines, then thirty-two fifty, then thirty-five hundred. When we get into the Davis Mountains we'll see fifty-six hundred-foot peaks. Right here we come to the end of Interstate Twenty."

Birch refolded her map and put Ace in the plane. "Ace is such a satisfactory dog, because he respects my moods. If I'm tired, his tail sags. If I'm happy, he jumps all over me. If I'm half asleep, like right now, he acts like he is too." She climbed in the front seat, put on her earphones, buckled her belt.

"Pop, can I taxi out? I've never taxied."

"Not if you're half asleep you can't."

"It'll wake me up. Anyway, I want to do it when there's nobody around to scorn me. What do I do?"

"Well, you taxi with your feet. If you want to go left, you press the left rudder pedal. If you want to go right—"

"I know. I press the right rudder pedal. Hurry and crank up so I can taxi."

"Brakes and contact?"

"Brakes. Contact!"

He swung the prop and the engine purred. He climbed in. "Give it a little gas to get it going. We'll be taking off on runway one-two."

The throttle was on the left sidewall. Birch eased it forward and the Cub started to roll.

"I'm going to turn here and taxi to the runway." She pressed the right rudder. Nothing happened. She pressed harder. The Cub moved slightly to the right.

"Pop, I'm pressing the pedal as hard as I can but the plane won't turn."

"Sometimes you have to give it a little right brake."

"How do I do that?"

"Press all the way down on your rudder pedal with your toes. Then push with your heel on the brake."

"Like this? Oh, we turned. Pop, we turned but not enough. We're going in the grass! Maybe you better taxi the rest of the way."

"You have to remember that a plane is not an automobile," Pop said. He taxied easily to the end of runway twelve. He checked for traffic. Then he said, "Want to take off?"

"Is it easier than taxiing?"

"Yes."

"So what do I do?"

"It'll take itself off if you let it. You ease the throttle all the way forward. It'll start down the runway. Try to stay in the center using your feet on the rudder pedals—I'll help you with that. When you start to pick up speed, ease the stick forward slightly. That'll lift the tail off. Then when the front wheels leave the runway, hold some back pressure and climb. I'll help you."

Birch took the throttle in her left hand and slowly pushed the knob forward. She felt a tingling in her spine. It was an all-out, wide-open, go-for-broke feeling. "Yahoo!"

With a roar, the Cub started down the runway and picked up speed. Birch eased the control stick forward a little. The tail came up. It seemed a long time until the front wheels left the hard runway and the J-3 climbed into the smooth air.

"Pop, look down there quick!"

"What?"

"At the end of the runway. Quick! It's a duck pond and there's a doghouse for ducks!"

"Birch, if you're going to fly the plane—"

"I am, but I know you're flying with me. I could feel your hand on the control. Anyway, it didn't seem to want to take off for me."

"You did fine. The air's thinner because of the elevation. So it takes longer to get off."

"You mean the higher up you are, the worse the plane flies."

"That's about it."

"You finish climbing, Pop, and then I'll fly for a while."

The air was calm. Below, the shadow of the J-3 moved across yucca-covered ranch land.

"See that access road on either side of the interstate?"

"Yes."

"We could land on that if we had to."

"Well, I hope we don't have to." She looked down at her map. "That little town right ahead must be Pyote. It's got the kind of four-legged water towers you see in western movies. All the other water towers we've seen were round and modern and advertised the high school football team—Bear Cubs . . . Panthers . . ."

They flew the distance from Pyote to Pecos in silence.

On either side of the road were fields with pale

circles where oil storage tanks had sat in better days. The only green spot was north of Pecos where a rancher had trees and a swimming pool. South of town was an old Air Force base with only the foundations of the buildings left, the long runways disappearing into the weeds.

Birch shook her head. "There wasn't a single house between Pyote and Pecos, did you notice, just some red and white towers. You know what I wanted to ask you about?"

"What's that?"

"On my map it says 'Street Patterns,' and out in the middle of nowhere, there are a whole bunch of lines, like streets."

"Oh, somebody probably laid the streets out and sold mail-order lots and people who didn't know any better sent in their money."

Birch was looking out the window. "Western towns can't hide anything, can they, Pop? It's all right out in the open, where they dump their garbage, where they play their football games. Should we have stopped at Pecos for gas? There's not an airport for miles."

"With any luck, we can make Van Horn, if not, we can land on the access road."

"Pop, you're looking for an excuse to land on that access road."

"I'm not, it's just comforting to know I can. I'll fly for a while."

Birch pulled her yellow visor low over her eyes. There wasn't much to see. There were a few towns along the interstate, but they had a shut-down look. To the north were the rugged crests of the Apache Mountains, to the south, the forest-crowned peaks of the Davis Mountains.

"We're climbing up out of the Pecos River Basin now," Pop commented.

Birch nodded. Her eyes were closed. She awoke an hour later with a start.

The first thing she saw was the gas gauge. The wire was bumping the bottom again. She pulled off her eyeshade and spun around. "Where are we?"

"About twenty-five miles from Van Horn."

"Are we going to make it?"

He shook his head.

"Not again!"

She faced forward and pulled herself up on the support bars. "So where are we going to land? Not that access road. I knew it. You're been dying to land on that access road ever since you saw it."

"There's not a thing wrong with that little stretch right down there."

"Pop—"

"And there's a truck stop . . . We could land right into the wind. We'll roll a little longer because the elevation here's about four thousand, but there's plenty of road."

"I can't believe we're doing this. Last night you were talking about being so careful and not taking any risks and how important it—Pop!"

"I can't hear you. You aren't speaking into the tube."

She whipped off her earphones and spun around. "You can too hear me."

"Don't talk. I'm busy." They flew above the access road, turned and circled back. Pop cut the throttle. Birch gripped the support bars and closed her eyes.

She could feel the plane bank as it turned on final approach to land. She glanced over the side. They were so close to the truck stop, she could read the names of the trucks. Then the plane sank slowly and settled with a bounce onto the access road.

They came to a stop and Pop said calmly, "Now I'll taxi to the truck stop and get some gas. Why don't you go in and get us some hamburgers?"

Pop and Birch walked to the truck stop—Pop to the gas pumps, Birch into the cafe.

She sat at the counter. "I can't believe this is happening to me," she said to the waitress.

"What, hon?"

"Did you see us land on that access road? That was us in that airplane. We just landed right outside your window."

"Well, I missed that."

"Everybody did, and if they didn't miss it, they just went, 'Well, there's an airplane landing on the road.' Nobody batted an eye, and we taxied across those cattle guards, and people go, 'Well, there's an airplane taxiing across cattle guards.' Our plane's parked right down there. You can see it if you look."

"Well, it sure is."

Birch shook her head. "Nothing bothers you people in Texas, does it?"

"Not much," the waitress said.

"I wish I was like that," Birch answered.

CHAPTER 17

Crabbing Over New Mexico

 ''POP, YOU KNOW what you forgot to do yesterday?''

It was day five. Pop and Birch had taken off from Las Cruces, New Mexico, at 7:28 and were now flying toward Lordsburg.

''What?''

''You forgot to call out, 'New Mexico!' when we passed El Paso.''

''Did I?''

''Yes, you were probably worn out from flying over El Paso. Pop, I don't want to exaggerate, so how long were we over El Paso?''

''Forty-five minutes.''

''How high were we?''

"Five hundred feet."

"I believe that because I could actually read the road signs. Next Exit—Las Cruces.

"I actually know every brick and bush in El Paso," she went on, "and there was not one place to land. El Paso has everything in the world but a place to land. The only possibility was, like, the Sun Bowl. Pop, where would we have landed if the engine had quit?"

"Well, it didn't, did it? We made it to Las Cruces."

"But if it had? Would you have landed across the Rio Grande in Mexico? There were some nice fields over there. I always have wanted to visit Mexico."

"Nope."

"Why not?"

"I'd rather crash in the United States."

"Well, I wouldn't. Why?"

"Birch, will you be quiet for five minutes."

"Yes, after I say one thing about Deming. That's Deming up ahead. Deming has more billboards leading into it than any city so far."

Silence.

"You know what my favorite billboards are?"

Silence.

"Those that advertise *The Thing*. Ninety miles to *The Thing*. Don't miss *The Thing*. Pop, what do you think the thing is?"

"I have no idea."

Birch turned around and looked at him. "Pop, I am sitting up here feeling so good and talking my head off and you're going, 'What? . . . Nope. I have no idea?' So what are you worried about?"

"What makes you think I'm worried?"

"Every time you get stingy with words, I know you're worried."

He worked up a smile. "I'm not worried exactly, but I'm not fond of this head wind."

"Head wind?" Birch looked out the window. "We have a head wind?"

"Actually it's a crosswind."

"That's why all the dust is blowing across the road," she said. She was just beginning to get a feeling for the powerful forces in the air.

Pop said, "Yes."

"It was so calm when we took off. I thought it was going to be a beautiful day. Now there are crosswinds. What happened?"

"The forecast said the winds would be out of the southwest—it's just stronger than they said."

"And I especially wanted to go fast today. I figured out yesterday—you know those big maps they have on the walls at airports? With the neat little string so you can measure how far you've got to go? Well, I measured at Las Cruces and we only have seven hundred more miles. I figured two good days and we'd be there."

"Look down on the ground."

"What am I looking for?" She leaned against the window.

"See the shadow of the plane?"

"Yes, I love shadows from the air. That's how I look for other planes. Like when we're going through a controlled area, the radio will say, 'Three six two, traffic at two o'clock, three miles,' and I look on the ground—for the shadow! Like, look at the telephone poles. The shadows make them look ten times as tall as they are."

"Look at our shadow," he said.

"Oh, I see what you're getting at. Out shadow's at an angle to the road."

"This is what's called crabbing. You've seen a crab going along the beach, haven't you, sort of sideways?"

"Yes."

"That's what we're having to do because of the crosswind."

"You don't like to crab?"

He smiled. "I don't like to land with a crosswind. It's hard to keep the Cub straight on the runway. It wants to ground loop."

"I know what that is—it's like a wheelie."

"I did one ground loop in the service, and the whole landing gear had to be replaced."

"I don't want to waste time replacing things, so let's don't ground loop."

"I'm going to try not to."

Birch looked at her map. "Where are we going to land?"

"The road's turning south now, and we're going to cut straight across and land at Lordsburg. It's an east-west runway, which is bad, but there's a dirt strip

121

into the wind—the Flight Guide calls it Dirt-ruf. Maybe we can land on that."

"I hate to leave the road, don't you?" Birch said. She watched the trucks and cars grow smaller. "It's like leaving civilization."

"We'll be following the pipeline."

"A pipeline is not civilization."

Birch leaned against the window. The land below was sandy, barren except for cactus and sagebrush. Ahead, the sharp peaked hills were blue against the morning sky.

Neither of them spoke.

They crossed a dry creek bed. The plane was so low that Birch could make out animal tracks in the pale sand. "Cow tracks and some little ones," she commented, "jackrabbits or lizards."

"The Continental Divide's along here somewhere," her grandfather said.

"Well, I'm glad there's something along here. Is this a desert?"

"It doesn't quite qualify."

"Why not? It's desolate enough. Oh, look there's a house—what do people do way out here in the middle of nowhere?"

"Live."

"Well, that's obvious."

She leaned against the window to look at the gray, weathered house. The cows in the creek bed were so dusty they blended into the ground.

"See the windmill," Pop said. "That tells you something about the wind."

"I would never have noticed that, Pop. You pay attention to things like which way smoke is blowing and what way clothes are blowing on the line and how waves are blowing on lakes. You notice a lot of things, Pop. You're—what's the word I want? Sensitive, I guess, though you're more than that.

"You know, when we started on this trip, there was something I wanted you to tell me, and I couldn't ask. I wasn't ready. And then when I talked to my dad on the phone, he said he'd talk to me when I got home. Which relieved me.

"And then I realized, Pop, that I was relieved partly because I wanted to hear it from you—whatever it was. Because I am probably closer to you than I am to anybody else in the world. And if you told me, I would take it better. I mean that as a compliment."

Pop said, "What are you muttering about up there?"

"Oh, nothing. I was paying you a compliment."

"I'd like to hear it when we get down from here."

Birch nodded. "I'd like to tell you—when we get down from here." She and Pop fell silent then.

They passed another creek bed, and Birch checked the tracks. "More jackrabbits, cows, I swear I see horned toad prints."

The foothills were seamed with dry washes now. Stunted shrubs had collected in the deep wrinkles.

"Well, do you feel better?" Pop said. "We're meeting back up with the interstate."

"I'd forgotten about that." She looked up at the line of traffic in the distance, no bigger now than a string of beads. "Yes, I do feel better. I like company."

"And that's Lordsburg ahead. I'm going to call them on the radio and see if it's safe to land on the dirt."

CHAPTER 18

Crosswind Miracle

 ''WELL, EVEN I KNOW it's windy when the wind sock is sticking out like a pole,'' Birch said.

"Be quiet," Pop said.

He turned on his radio and set the frequency. "Lordsburg Unicom, Piper Cub three oh three six two."

"Plus, we are the only fools in the air. I have not seen one other plane."

Pop waited. When there was no answer, he said again, "Lordsburg Unicom, how do you hear Piper Cub three oh three six two?"

"They've probably closed up and gone home," Birch muttered to herself.

A voice from the radio said, "Cub three six two, Lordsburg. Hear you five square now. Go ahead."

"Lordsburg, Cub three six two is ten miles east, over the interstate, landing Lordsburg. Say wind and traffic and what is the condition of runway one-nine?"

"Cub three six two, wind is two zero zero at about twenty knots, gusting to twenty-five or thirty, favoring runway one-nine. No reported traffic. Runway one-nine is dirt but condition is good. No problem for a Cub. Over."

"Roger, Lordsburg. We'll be coming up on left base for one nine in a couple of minutes. Keep me posted if there is any significant wind change."

"Rog, three six two."

"It looks all right," her grandfather said.

"How fast is twenty knots?"

"Don't talk to me now."

"Well, it's my life too!"

"Between twenty-five and thirty miles an hour!"

They approached the airport in silence. Pop turned the J-3 on final. He said into the radio, "Lordsburg traffic, Cub three six two turning final for one nine."

Birch could see the runway below—dirt with yellow arrows on the edge made out of automobile tires.

"Belt tight?" he asked.

"You bet."

Now that they were heading directly into the wind, the J-3 hardly seemed to be moving over the ground at all. As the plane began to sink toward the runway, the turbulent air coming over the hills to the west began to bounce the plane around.

Birch reached for the support bars and held on tight. Behind her Ace barked in sharp protest.

The J-3 touched down on the hard earth once, twice, and finally a third time. Then it slowed to a stop at the intersection to the ramp.

"Now the fun begins," Pop said tensely.

"What? We're down!"

"We've got to turn one hundred ten degrees to the ramp. It's one thing when the wind is blowing straight toward us, but when we turn and that wind gets under the wing—Birch, you better get out and hold it."

"What? The airplane?"

"Hold onto the wingtip and steady it."

"Pop, I weigh one hundred pounds. I couldn't hold an airplane down, especially if the wind wanted to take it up."

She undid her seat belt and climbed out. "Now I have done everything," she mumbled. She went carefully around the back of the airplane, as Pop had taught her, and took the left wingtip.

As the plane started around the corner, the wind gusted and tried to lift it. Birch opened her mouth to scream as the wing picked her up on her toes.

"I've got it," a voice said in her ear.

Birch whipped her hair from her eyes and turned. A boy was behind her. His hand stretched around hers onto the wingtip. It was a miracle. Even if it had been an ugly boy, it would have been a miracle, but this boy was not ugly.

Birch was aware she could let go, but she didn't. Together the two of them walked the J-3 around the corner, guiding it to the ramp.

Pop cut the engine and said, "Let's get this thing tied down before the wind blows it over."

A man with a sun-cured face came out to help them, but the boy already had the left wing tied down. His movements had a western quickness, like something out of a rodeo, Birch thought.

"It's too much wind for me," Pop told the man.

"For me too," Birch told the boy. "I bet we were the only people in the air today."

"The only ones we've seen."

The boy moved to the right wing. Birch moved with him. "Even our dog—this is Ace—" Birch reached into the cockpit.

"Hello, Ace." The boy paused to scratch him behind one ear.

"It was even too much for Ace. He barked for the first time since we left South Carolina."

The boy finished the right wing and moved to the tail of the plane. Birch went along.

"You folks are from South Carolina?" he asked.

"Yes, where are *you* from?"

"Here."

"Oh."

"You folks planning to spend the night in Lordsburg?" the man asked.

Birch said quickly, "I am. I promised myself that if I got down safely, I wasn't going to get back in the airplane today." She looked at Pop.

He said, "I pretty much promised myself the same thing." He took off his glasses and blotted his face on his sleeve.

"My son'll be glad to drive you to a motel."

"We'd appreciate it." Pop looked at his watch. "Birch, it's only nine o'clock in the morning. What are we going to do all day?"

Birch glanced at the boy. The dry hot wind seemed to be blowing them together. "Oh, I don't know . . . recover."

The man said, "Pete, get the car and drive these folks into town."

"I'll be right back."

Pop checked the ropes again, and Birch said, "Pop, that boy—Pete—tied them perfectly. He—"

Pop looked up. "Where'd Ace get to? Ace!"

A mouse-colored dog with a flea collar was disappearing around the hangar. Ace was trotting behind, trying to get the dog's attention.

"That'll do, Ace," Pop said.

Birch ran after Ace and scooped him up. "That dog's too big for you. You're not in her league." She brought Ace back to the J-3.

In the parking lot, the boy was starting an old station wagon.

"Pop," she said, "you know what worries me when

we have a day like today—or yesterday?" She grinned. "Or the day before that?"

"What?"

"That we're going to have to turn around and go home. We're going to do it all over again, only the other way. Like, we'll hang over El Paso for forty-five minutes again, we'll go over those Van Horn mountains, we'll land on that access road, we'll—"

"The reason we're flying so low is because of the head winds. The higher we get, the stronger the winds are. On the way home, we'll have tail winds. We'll be at five thousand feet instead of five hundred. You won't even recognize it as the same place."

"Is that a promise?" She broke off as the station wagon stopped beside them. "I'll ride in the front with Pete," Birch said quickly. "You and Ace just sit in the back and relax."

CHAPTER 19

Seven Lines

 ''POP, DO YOU REALIZE that this is the first date I've ever had in my life," Birch said.

Pop was watching the Weather Channel so he didn't react. "Look at those winds," he said, shaking his head. "No wonder we had trouble."

"And it's with a cute boy. Don't you think he's cute, Pop?"

"What?"

"Don't you think Pete's cute?"

"Pete?"

"The boy! *The* boy! The one I have a date with!"

Now she had his attention.

"You didn't say anything about a date. You said you were going to a movie."

"That's what a date is, Pop—going to a movie. I can't wait to write my best friend BiBi. Bibi's had a date, but his mother drove them. His mother kept spying on them in the rearview mirror."

"I don't know what your mother's going to say about a date."

"Do you think I look fifteen? That's how old I told him I was."

"You ain't but thirteen." Pop looked as bewildered as if he'd begun to lose track of the years.

"I couldn't say I was just thirteen because he has to be sixteen to drive."

"You're going in the car?"

"Yes, Pop, I wish you'd had some other kind of shampoo besides Tegrin. I'm afraid he's going to smell Tegrin in my hair and think I have dandruff."

"How's he going to smell your hair?"

"And I wish I had something else to wear!"

She overturned her knapsack and shook out the contents. Some underwear, a T-shirt, and a box of poems fell onto the bed. She reached out to replace the box, then changed her mind and left it where it was.

"Your mom is not going to approve of any date. I know she's not."

"Oh, Pop."

"That's why you didn't mention having a date when you called home."

"Oh, Pop."

"You knew she wouldn't approve. Does she let you go out on dates at home?"

"It's never come up. Nobody's ever asked me. Oh, that's his station wagon. Pop, he's here. Now please, please don't say anything to embarrass me."

"Birch, you behave yourself."

"Like that! That's exactly the kind of thing I don't want you to say."

"And don't you be late."

"I won't. Pop, you're acting like a mother hen. I promise you have nothing to worry about."

"I can't help it."

As Birch waited for the knock on the motel room door, she said, "You know what I wish, Pop? I wish tomorrow would be windy and the next day and the day after that. I wish we'd be stuck in Lordsburg a whole week. By that time Pete and I could be going steady."

Pop straightened in alarm. "Steady?"

"Pop, do these jeans look all right with this shirt?"

"Birch, quit rattling on."

"I can't help it. I'm nervous. I know the shirt doesn't look good with the jeans, but these are the only clean things I've got. Oh, what am I going to talk about?"

"Talk about airplanes."

"Tell me one thing to say that's not stupid, and I'll feel better."

"Ask him if he's a pilot."

"Then what?"

"Ask him how long he's been one—what kind of plane he flies. I could talk to pilots all day."

"Why isn't he knocking? I know I heard his station wagon backfiring. What's he doing out there?"

She pulled the curtain aside and shut it with a gasp. "Oh, Pop, he was combing his hair, and he saw me looking. Oh, Pop, I could just die. And he looks super —a hundred times better than I do. He's probably getting back in the car. He's probably leaving!"

There was a knock at the door. Birch took a deep breath and opened it. She smiled. "Hi."

"Hi."

Birch said quickly, "We're going, Pop."

"Well, don't you be late, Birch. If the wind lets up, I want to take off early tomorrow morning."

"I won't. Maybe you should give me the room key, Pop, so I won't disturb you when I come in."

"I'll be up," he said firmly.

Birch closed the door, and she and Pete crossed the parking lot to the station wagon. Birch swallowed again and said, "By the way, I meant to ask you this afternoon—are you a pilot?"

"No, I just hang around the airport because of my dad."

"Oh."

"Are you one?"

"No, I fly sometimes when my grandfather wants a break, but you couldn't call me a pilot."

"Oh."

Birch was beginning to hate that word. They got in

the station wagon, and Pete combed his hair again while Birch swallowed.

"You know what my favorite signs are from the air?" she asked in desperation.

"Signs?"

"Yes, you know, like, billboards. We fly so low that I can read billboards."

"Oh."

"My favorites are *The Thing*. Ninety miles to *The Thing*. Don't miss *The Thing*. I'd love to know what *The Thing* is."

"A two-headed lizard."

"What?"

"A two-headed lizard. It's pickled."

"Are you kidding?"

"No, that's what my cousin told me. She says it's a big gyp."

"I am so glad you told me that. Now I won't mind missing it one bit."

Birch swirled into the motel room. Pop had fallen asleep on his bed, but he roused. "What time is it? What time is it?"

"Four o'clock in the morning."

"What?"

"I was teasing. It's ten-thirty." She sat down on the bed. Her hand dropped to her side, touching the box of poems, which lay as it had fallen from her backpack.

"I had a good time, Pop."

"Did you behave yourself?"

"Yes." She took the lid off the box. "Pop, would you like to hear one of Granny's poems?"

"Is that what you've been carrying around in that box?"

"Yes. You want to hear one?"

"I reckon not."

"Why not?"

"I never would listen to them when she was alive. I don't reckon I got any right to listen now."

"Yes, you do. And—oh, here's one of my favorites, Pop. And at the top it says 'For Earl' so I know she's talking about you. Can I read it?"

"I guess I can't stop you."

> *"I would have known you*
> *Any place*
> *I would have recognized*
> *Your face*
> *Would have stretched my hand*
> *To trace*
> *The kind line of your smile."*

There was a silence, and Birch let it stand. She took a deep breath without breaking the stillness.

"That's a poem that doesn't have any, well, mystery to it. What Granny's saying is that no matter where she had seen you, she would have known that you were meant for her."

"I suppose."

"But sometimes, Pop, poems are mysterious. Take this one. Can I read it?"

"If it's not about me. I liked hearing the one, but that'll do me for now."

"It's not. I don't know who it's about.

She reached to the bottom of the box and brought out the last poem. She breathed in and out as if she needed to store up some air before she read.

> *The baby took one fluttering gasp*
> *Two . . .*
> *Three . . .*
> *Each softer than the last.*
> *Four . . .*
> *One more. . . .*
> *Passed. All past.*

She lay the poem with the others and looked down at them as she spoke.

"It was written on my birthday so it has something to do with me. I thought at first," she went on carefully, "that mom and dad's natural baby had died and I had maybe taken her place."

"You didn't take anybody's place."

"I know that now."

"Your mom ought to be the one talking to you about this."

"Mom isn't here. And I'm ready to hear it. Besides I want you to tell me."

"You ought to be able to figure it out," he said stubbornly avoiding it.

"I think I have, but I need to hear it."

Pop sighed. "Well, you were born and you were perfect—a big, beautiful baby girl. And while they were working on you, doing whatever it is they do to new babies, the doctor said, 'Well, it looks like there's another one.' "

Pop swallowed.

"This was a surprise even to the doctor and nurses."

He ran his hands through his hair and fell silent.

"And the second baby came," she prompted.

"Yes."

"And died."

"Yes. Oh, it was a little, bitty thing—two, three pounds at most."

Birch closed her eyes against the pain. She thought she had been ready to hear it, but she wasn't so sure now.

"Was it a boy or girl, Pop?"

"Girl."

"I guess she didn't have a chance, being so little."

"Little babies have lived before, Birch, but there was something else involved—about the heart. I don't remember the word for it. Your mom will know."

"Did they name her, Pop?"

"I believe they called her Clare."

"And her whole life could be put into one little short poem. Seven lines."

"I guess."

"Seven lines I'll remember for the rest of my life."
She closed the box of poems. "Thank you, Pop, for
telling me."

CHAPTER 20

The Thing

 IT WAS THE NEXT MORNING. Birch was in the front seat of the J-3.

"I feel good, Pop," she said, "and it isn't just because of the date. I have been dreading hearing about"—she paused—"Clare, and dreading it. I've even had nightmares. And now that I have heard it—and Pop, this is to your credit. You told it in a very unhurtful way."

"Did I?"

"Yes, I didn't feel that you blamed me."

"Nobody blames you."

"But when someone that you genuinely admire doesn't blame you, then it makes it easier not to blame yourself.

"Anyway, now that I have heard it—well, you remember what you said before we left about the missing piece of the puzzle?"

"Sort of."

"You said Granny could never enjoy the puzzle if there was one piece missing. The one piece was everything. I can sympathize with that now. Because sometimes it's that one little piece that lets you see the whole picture."

She threw back her head. "I feel good enough to compose a poem!"

"I was afraid of that."

"When will I see Pete? Let me count the days.

"No," she decided, "Elizabeth Barrett Browning's way was better. I'll start over."

"Not on my account," Pop said.

"How do I love Pete? Let me count the ways.
I love him to the depth and breath and height
my soul can reach.
I love him with the passion of my girlhood and—"

"That's enough!" Pop said from the backseat. "I don't want any talk about passion."

"I was just trying to get a rise out of you," Birch answered calmly, "I'm tired of flying over Arizona."

"You got a rise, all right. I want you behaving yourself. No more dates for you."

"Oh, Pop, I'm just disappointed," Birch said. "I wanted some wind this morning. I had a wonderful,

wonderful time last night, and if we'd stayed over, I could probably have had another wonderful time. This was the, *the* first cute boy I've ever been able to talk to, and you drag me away."

"I wish we'd never stopped."

"Anyway, I told Pete we'd probably be back in about a week. I told him to—Oh, Pop, there it is!"

"What?"

"Where *The Thing* lives. Take a picture of it. Quick! Where's your camera?"

"I'm getting it."

Birch pressed her face against the left window. Below, curled on the top of the mountain like a dragon, was a rambling red, yellow, and blue building.

"And I found out what *The Thing* is. Pop, it's—"

"Turn your head around so you'll be in the picture too."

"Gladly. I'll send him a copy." Birch posed. She said, "I found out last night—from Pete, the wonderful, wonderful boy I went out with, that *The Thing*'s a two-headed pickled lizard."

"That figures."

"And look how they ruined that mountain. That is an ugly, ugly building, which they built for a two-headed lizard."

"There's something pretty," Pop said. He pointed to a hawk that glided by in a graceful, sideways sweep. Its head was turned away, pointedly ignoring them.

"You won't see a prettier sight than that. Yonder's another one."

The Thing

"I imagined all our days would be like yesterday, Pop, relaxing at motels, me going out with cute boys . . . You know, I like western people; they're so laid back. Last night, Pete and I got a hamburger after the movie and there was this little girl—she was probably seven years old, and she was clomping around in high heels—they were not an old pair of her mom's. They were hers. Her grandmother goes, 'She's going to break her neck in them things,' and the mom just yawns. 'She's got to learn to walk in heels sometime.' Pop, you ought to be more western."

"It's too late for me."

"You could work at it. Like, the next time you hear thunder, don't hop up and run to the airport—Oh, Pop, pass Ace up here to me. I've been neglecting him."

Pop handed Ace into the front seat and Birch said, "Ace, let me tell you about my date. Pop's tired of hearing about it, but you are a better listener. Pete came for me in his father's station wagon about . . ."

They flew for a while and Pop said, "I hate to interrupt, but we're coming into the Tucson area. I need to talk on the radio."

Birch straightened and looked out the window. "Oh, I have wanted to see Tucson my entire life. Ace, that's Tucson!"

Pop cleared his throat and said, "Tucson approach, Piper Cub three oh three six two."

The radio answered, "Piper three oh three six two, Tucson. Go ahead."

"Tucson, Cub three six two is fifteen miles south of Tucson International, VFR at thirty-five hundred feet, northbound along I-ten to Phoenix, requesting flight following through your area. Negative transponder."

"What does that mean—negative transponder?" Birch asked.

"It means I don't have one."

"And VFR?"

"Birch—"

"Well, how am I ever going to learn?"

"VFR is Visual Flight Rules. It means we aren't on an instrument flight plan like most of the bigger planes in the area."

"Oh. Hey, I like Tucson," Birch said as the city came into view. "It looks like the kind of city that cares how it looks from the air—nice red roofs over here, nice blue roof on that real tall building, nice—"

The radio said, "Piper three six two, are you exactly over a rodeo fairground?"

Pop dipped one wing and looked. He said, "Piper three six two, that's affirmative."

"Roger, three six two, we have you. Radar contact."

"I know what that means," Birch said, "we are now an official dot on the radar screen."

The radio said, "Three six two, turn north and stay over I-ten. Maintain thirty-five hundred feet."

"Three six two, roger. Turning north."

In silence Birch watched the scenery below. West of the city giant saguaroa and organ pipe cacti stood

144

stiffly on the jagged bronze hills. On the mountain someone had painted a big white A.

Birch couldn't help herself. She blurted out, "Those letters everybody puts on mountains do one thing—ruin a perfectly good mountain."

"Birch!"

"My mouth is closed for the rest of the flight. But, Pop, remind me to tell you something about Tucson's garbage."

"Go ahead and tell me."

"It's blue. Tucson has blue garbage! Look at the dump!" She pointed. "See, Pop! Could we fly over there and get a closer look?"

"You know we can't. You heard the radio tell us to stay over the interstate."

"But why, why would Tucson have blue garbage? I'm going to wonder about that the rest of my life." Suddenly she threw back her head. "Oh, Pop, it is just so, *so* good—the best feeling in the entire world!"

"What?"

"That all I have to wonder about is blue garbage!" She broke off. "Anyway, I see you inching over to look at those surplus warplanes. Why can we go look at your garbage when we can't go over and check out mine?"

CHAPTER 21

Down, Down in the Valley

"I LOVE CALIFORNIA! Pop, I love it."

It was 2:45 in the afternoon, and the J-3 Cub had just left the airport at Blythe, California. Their other stops had been Tucson and Phoenix.

Birch twisted around in her seat. "You know what I thought when I first saw it?"

"Nope."

"We were coming over those Arizona mountains, and they weren't all that high, but we were low. And it was bumpy, Pop, and I was afraid on one of those bumps we'd sink down too far and hit."

"We didn't."

"And then, Pop, then we went over the last barren,

146

brown peak and suddenly, suddenly there was this beautiful green valley. It was the first green I'd seen since the Sun Bowl. And a river too! And palm trees taller than telephone poles! And canals! It took my breath away.

"You yelled, 'California,' and a poem popped into my mind. This particular poem had never popped into my mind before—see, poems pop into my mind when I feel the exact way the poet did. Like the other day when we left the road, what popped into my mind was 'I wandered lonely as a cloud that floats on high o'er blah . . . blah . . . blah.

"But this poem by Edna St. Vincent Millay–I've had it memorized for two whole years and I've been waiting and waiting for something wonderful to happen to me—I don't count my date—that was wonderful but not in the same way. You want me to say the poem for you?"

"By all means."

> *"And as I looked a quickening gust*
> *Of wind blew up to me and thrust*
> *Into my face a miracle*
> *Of orchard-breath, and with the smell,*
> *—I know not how such things can be!—*
> *I breathed my soul back into me."*

There was a silence. Birch sighed. "Did you feel like that, Pop?"

"Well, I was mighty glad to see Blythe, California and the Colorado River."

"Edna St. Vincent Millay wasn't a lot older than me when she wrote that— Oh, are we leaving the inter- state again? We aren't going across those mountains, are we? I haven't even opened my California map."

She unfolded it and turned it around. "I don't have the foggiest idea where we are."

He leaned over her shoulder and put his thumbnail on a yellow area. "Well, there's Blythe."

"You know what I thought was neat, Pop. At the Blythe airport you asked the lady where we could get something to eat and she told us to taxi over to the truck stop. So we got in the plane, taxied to the truck stop, got out, ate, got back in the plane and took off."

Pop said, "We're right here. We're going to leave our old standby I-ten and cut across Eagle Mountain, Joshua Tree National Monument, and the Pinto Mountains. We'll spend the night right there at Twenty-nine Palms."

"Now this *is* desert we're crossing over because I see it on the map. That's Desert Center right down there."

"This land's the same as it was a hundred years ago when the old Bradshaw freight wagons crossed it . . . Except I don't reckon that mine was there."

Birch pulled herself forward with the support bars to look.

"They call that Alligator Mountain," Pop said. "You can see why."

"Oh, look what they've done to that mountain. They've ruined it. Look, Pop."

"I see."

"It's like something out of *Star Wars*. They're cutting away the whole, entire mountain. I hate to see things like that. And that huge pile of dirt looks like it came out of a Jello mold. It's so ugly."

She watched the mine intently, then turned to Pop. "I got so upset about them ruining that mountain that I forgot to be scared going over it. Are these the San Gabriel Mountains, the ones I'm worried about?"

"No, they'll be the last ones before the Pacific."

"Are they worse than these?"

"That's what they say."

"You know what else I hate? I hate to see water that looks like melted ice cream—like lime or pistachio or buttered almond because water is supposed to look like one thing—water!"

She turned indignantly to the front of the plane. Then she fell silent. She felt as if she were looking at a planet that had just died.

There, stretching ahead of the plane, lay a broad, bone-dry valley, fenced in by mountains as barren as crumpled brown wrapping paper. Birch blinked. There was not a trace that a person had ever been here—not a tire track, not a footprint, not the glint of metal. She leaned forward in grim wonder.

"Pop, it's like somebody leaned down with a giant eraser and just went over everything." Pop was silent.

"Pop, what if we had to land out here? Nobody would ever find us."

"We'd have a walk, all right. But remember we have a radio. We could call for help."

"Pop, I can't get over this. You know, every single place we've flown over, even the most deserted, there was always some sign of life, like a tire track or an abandoned shack, oil wells or pipe lines. Here there is nothing. And it's huge."

"The valley's only about fifteen or twenty miles across, but when you're only making fifty-two miles an hour, it'll take a while."

She leaned against the window, looking at the barren ground. "I guess I should be glad that there's some place in the United States people haven't found yet . . ."

"Birch, do you see that tiny threadlike line in the hills ahead."

She squinted at the distant, ragged black hills. "Yes."

"I'm trying to figure out if that's a road."

"I think so." She looked down. "Pop, even dune buggies haven't found this place."

Pop said, "Yes, that's a road. Right beside it is a sort of mom-and-pop mine, a shoestring operation."

Birch peered at the raw, unpainted board shacks, the rusting tin roofs. "No trucks, no people. I never see any people. I guess mom and pop gave up."

"I guess."

"Oh, Pop, look! There's—" She broke off. "Oh, it's

another mine. It looked like the ruins from cliff dwellers for a minute. I mean if it wasn't for the tons and tons of spillage below it."

She shook her head in dismay. "I always had a thing about cliff dwellers and just for a moment, before I saw the spillage, I got excited." She trailed off.

"I guess their mothers didn't teach them to fill up a hole when they got through digging it," Pop said. "Mine sure did."

"Mine, too. You know what, Pop?"

"What's that?"

"The California of my poem—the California that breathed my soul back into me—didn't seem to last but about fifteen minutes."

CHAPTER 22

Wings Over the San Gabriel Mountains

 "MOM, HI, IT'S ME."

"Birch! Why didn't you call last night?"

"I did! Well, I tried about fourteen times, and the line was busy. Pop kept saying, 'Try again, try again.' And finally I said, 'Why are you so eager for me to get Mom? All you ever tell her is that we used one hundred and sixty-one gallons of gas.' He said, 'Well, maybe I've got something else to say this time.' I go, 'What?' He said, 'I'm not going to sell this airplane, that's what.' I wasn't supposed to tell you that."

"I knew that was going to happen."

"I didn't, but it made me real happy, because it just seemed cruel to sell the plane after it flew us all the way to California!"

"He's probably changed his mind about the retirement home as well."

"Yes, that too."

"Where are you, Birch?"

"I'm at a pay phone at Apple Valley Air Lodge right now, but last night we stayed at a wonderful place called Twenty-nine Palms. Mom, it was beautiful with huge old palm trees and cottonwoods. The inn had four dogs—two were Saint Bernards, and they let Ace be in the pack. Mom, Ace has made millions of friends, and guess what!"

"Slow down, Birch."

"I can't. Pop's waving at me to come. Oh, he wanted me to tell you we went four hundred ten miles yesterday and used twenty-seven and two tenths gallons of gas. Anyway, last night we could hear coyotes, Mom, real coyotes. The lady said they come in the garden to eat melons. I go, 'I didn't know coyotes ate melons.' She goes, 'Oh, yes, there's a green gourd that grows in the desert called the coyote melon because they like it so much. They eat it and yowl.' "

Birch shifted her weight and gave Pop an 'I'm coming' wave.

"I've got to tell you one more thing. We're getting ready to go over the big mountains. The San Gabriels. We've been over some terrible mountains, but these are supposed to be the worst. I started worrying about them way back in Texas. But after we landed here, Pop asked the man about where was the best way to cross, and the man said, 'It's easy. I'll show you.' He's German, I'll do his accent. It was a shock when I first heard him on the radio. He said, 'Haff a safe landing.' That didn't sound like him, but you get the idea.

"Anyway, Pop asked him about crossing the mountains. Pop said, 'Wait, I'll get my map.' The man said, 'You don't need a map, chust stay to the rrright of the mountains. Take the second walley—not the walley the rrrailrrroad goes through—the next one. You shoult be able to see this airport and this lake . . .'

"Anyway, he made it sound easy but I don't believe him. Oh, I really do have to go now. Pop's got his hands on his hips. I'll call you tonight."

"Birch," her mother said, "you sound . . . better."

"I am better, Mom. I'll tell you about it tonight."

Birch hung up the phone and ran across the ramp. "I'm sorry I took so long, Pop, but you know Mom. She has to hear every detail."

Pop took off his glasses and blotted the sweat from his face onto his sleeve. "Well, we can't put it off any longer. Get in. The takeoff roll's going to be a long one—this field's one of the highest so far."

Pop set the altimeter on 3390, and they taxied to the end of runway 21. They rolled and finally lifted off the ground. Birch watched the San Gabriel Mountains as the J-3 climbed slowly toward them. Clouds were forming over the peaks. The mountains seemed to grow as they got closer.

She said, "When I look at mountains like that, I get a new respect for pioneers, don't you?"

Pop didn't answer. Birch checked the altimeter. They were at 5000. The Cub was beginning to labor.

"What's the name of the pass we're going through?"

"Soledad. Watch for a four-lane road. See that white dot on the mountain?"

"Yes."

"I think that's the place we turn in."

"Oh, there's some black, coffee-colored water, the kind I hate." Suddenly Birch grabbed the support bar. "Pop, it's getting bumpy."

"There'll be turbulence."

"I don't mind bobbing up under the clouds. I hate sinking down later. Like that!"

The compass sung wildly back and forth. Birch checked her seat belt again. Ace barked sharply in protest.

Pop shot a nervous look up at the mountains on the left. "I don't care for the downwind side of the mountain."

"Why, Pop?"

"The upwind side lifts you up, helps you. The downwind side—" He broke off. "Oh, that's where the railroad goes through. We don't take that pass. We want the next valley to the left." All his thoughts seemed to be on not cutting through the mountains too quickly.

Birch checked the altimeter. They were at 6000 feet

now, close to the base of the clouds. The peaks of the San Gabriels rose still higher.

"There's another plane, Pop. And that white dot on the mountain you mentioned is a house with an antenna. Things are so disappointing—you see an interesting white dot and it's a house. You see a glistening castle and it turns out to be a power plant. Cliff dwellings turn out to be—"

"Don't talk so much, Birch."

"I always talk when I'm nervous, you ought to know that by now."

"Well, I don't like to listen when I'm nervous. I'll feel better when I can see that lake the man was talking about. You don't see a lake, do you?"

Birch strained forward. "No."

"I was afraid of that. How about an airport?" He pushed his map over her shoulder. His thumb marked one of the magenta circles.

Body rigid, she strained forward again. "No."

"Well, keep looking."

Birch hugged herself. She looked at the slopes below. It was as if somebody had pulled up the cloth of the earth and then let it drop back down in folds. Some peaks were as smooth as the plastic ones in model railroad villages. Roads wiggled through the brown hills. Small red-roofed developments were set in the deepest wrinkles.

"There's the four-lane road," Pop said. "Here we go!"

156

In one breathtaking moment they cut through the mountains, and Birch saw the valley beyond.

The air was rougher. Birch held on with both hands. Ace barked a series of high barks.

"There's an amusement park. That ought to be on the map." He shook his head. ". . . but it's not."

"All these valleys and interstates look alike. I don't know why that man said it was so easy."

There were mountains on either side of them. Below, irregular-shaped fields lay in bends of the road. A riverbed twisted beside the highway.

"Now, that river *is* on the map. I see it. We're right, Pop."

"I believe we are."

"I never did see the lake though."

"Me either."

"It's getting smoother." She glanced at the ground. "They ought to call this condo valley—look at all those houses crammed together. No wonder they have mud slides . . . Have we got a head wind? We sure are going slow."

"We aren't going slow at all. We're going seventy miles an hour."

"It seems slow when you can't see any place you could land."

"That's right."

"The map's getting greener—that's a good sign. And the mountains are getting flatter."

Birch glanced at the altimeter. 3500 feet. They were descending. The fields reached up the sides of the

157

hills now. Every piece of land had been made into a field or a golf course.

They were at 2500 feet now. To Birch it was like floating down an invisible river, heading for the sea.

"There's the Santa Paula airport!" Pop said. "We'll land there. I've been looking forward to this. There's every kind of antique airplane in the world there."

"Just what I wanted to see—airplanes."

"It's a busy airport though. You help me watch for traffic."

"Well, there's a plane." Birch pointed. "And there's another one—at three o'clock," she added with a smile.

"I see that one."

"And there's one taking off and one getting ready to take off. Do they have a tower or do you just sort of get in line?" She broke off. "I know, I know, shut up so you can talk on the radio."

CHAPTER 23

A Victory Lap

 ''D o you see the Pacific?'' Pop asked.

Birch was leaning forward, peering over the cowling. "No! Why? Do you?'' She had been looking for the ocean ever since they took off from the Santa Paula airport fifteen minutes ago.

The Santa Paula canyon had opened into a broad valley. The city of Ventura was just ahead.

"I see it,'' Pop said.

"I don't see anything but haze! Pop, where is it?''

He pointed straight ahead with a long sunburned finger.

"Pop! I don't see it!''

"It sort of fades into the sky.''

"I know it's there, but I can't see it! Oh, now I do. I think I do."

She sank back in her seat as if she were giving up. "This is not at all the way I dreamed it would be. I dreamed I'd see it and start screaming, 'I'm the first one to see the Pacific!'"

"Well, you weren't the first one to see the Pacific."

"I'm not even sure I see it now." She peered into the haze. "Yes, I do see some waves." She gave a mock scream. "I'm the second one to see the Pacific!"

"You want to fly on up the coast a little bit?"

"I want to do something," she said. "What's happened to me? I've been looking forward to getting here and looking forward to getting here and now I am here and I want to keep going. I wish the United States didn't stop. I wish there was some more of it."

"There is. Hawaii. It's out there somewhere."

"Pop, I'm serious. Do you feel sort of let down?"

"No, I believe this is the best I ever felt in my life." His lips curled in a smile. "I thought you'd be popping another poem."

"Why do you feel good and I feel let down?"

"I couldn't say. You want to fly up the coast?"

She nodded.

"We could go to—" He checked the map. "San Luis Obispo is a nice little town."

"Have we got enough gas to make it?"

"Yes."

"Then let's go."

They swung out over the Pacific. Below, the shadow

160

of the plane moved across the green water. "Now I'm sure it's the Pacific," Birch said, "because I see surfers down there. That makes me feel a little better."

"You know how race drivers always take an extra lap around the track, keep driving a little bit?" Pop said. "Well, this is our extra lap—our victory lap."

The window was open and Birch could smell the salt air. She rested her arm on the window, and let the roar of the engine flow over her.

"I'm glad you said that about the victory lap, Pop. And I must admit this is exactly the way I thought California beaches would look—surfers and movie star houses. Look at those houses on the cliff. One of them even has a cable car to get people down to the beach."

"That's Santa Barbara ahead. I'll give them a call on the radio."

Birch barely listened. She looked from side to side, taking it all in—the offshore oil rigs, a volleyball game on the beach below, the fishing boats, the white circling gulls, the long piers. It was as if she were seeing all these things for the first time.

"I didn't expect to see farms. And they go right to the edge of the cliff, Pop. California cows must have a lot of sense not to fall off."

The mountains beyond the farms were rocky, the vegetation between the rocks so dark it looked black. A white plane moved south just below the top of the ridge.

Another airplane always came as a shock to Birch,

because flying gave her the illusion that she and Pop were doing something nobody else in the world was doing. The sky seemed untraveled, new, unknown.

"We'll turn inland with the highway," Pop commented.

Birch glanced at the ocean. Far out to sea, clouds were forming. They seemed to curve with the bow of the earth.

Suddenly Birch flattened her map against her chest. She blinked back unexpected tears. The force of her emotion took her by surprise.

Even though the emotion had come unexpectedly, it came with such clarity that it was as if her mind had been working on it in secret, as if her mind had been waiting to spring this on her as a surprise.

She saw the trip in a new way, as a whole. She had crossed rivers and desert valleys, hopped mesas, crossed states without touching them, almost reached the clouds. She had seen garbage and incredible beauty. She had flown shoulder to shoulder with a hawk. The trip as a whole was what was important, just as she, with all the pieces in place, was more important than any single part.

And Pop! Pop was a new person. He could even make her laugh. The night before she had said, "Pop, did you know Granny had two pillows named Willow and Billow?"

"Yes, I am acquainted with Willow and Billow."

"Did they sleep with you and Granny?"

"Both of them did. But then Billow, or Willow—I

never could keep them straight, and if I mixed up their names, your grandmother took it as an insult. Anyway I'm pretty sure it was Billow that got washed with my work pants and I thought, well, good, now I'll just have to put up with Willow, but . . ." He broke off. "What are you laughing at?"

The feeling of happiness crept up on her like daybreak. She swallowed aloud.

"Do you feel a poem coming on?" Pop asked.

"No poem has popped in my mind, Pop, but I have the feeling that someday a poet will fly over this country like we did and write a poem about it and I'll come across it and . . ." She shrugged away the rest of the sentence. She was unable to finish.

"Send me a copy. Or, better still, why don't you write one yourself?"

"I thought you didn't like poetry."

"Well, I'd like that one."

Birch looked down at her map. She marked a place with her thumb.

"That tower is there, so we are here. I'm getting good at this," she said with satisfaction.

"It's called navigation," Pop said mildly.

"Our next checkpoint should be—" she gasped.

"What is it?"

"Oh, Pop, remember when we were talking about endangered species? Remember I said that's what the J-3 is? Well, look what it says on the map. Pop, I am so excited."

"About what?"

"Condor Sanctuary! We won't come close to it today, but maybe on the way home. 'Notice to pilots.
California condor (endangered species) nesting in the
Sespe Sanctuary . . .' Oh, I hope we see one. It
would be the first time I've ever seen anything endangered. Pop, you know what I think?"

Birch rested her hand on the control stick so she
could follow what Pop was doing.

"What's that?"

"I think the trip home's going to be even more exciting than the trip out."

"Could be," Pop said, starting their descent. "Could
be."

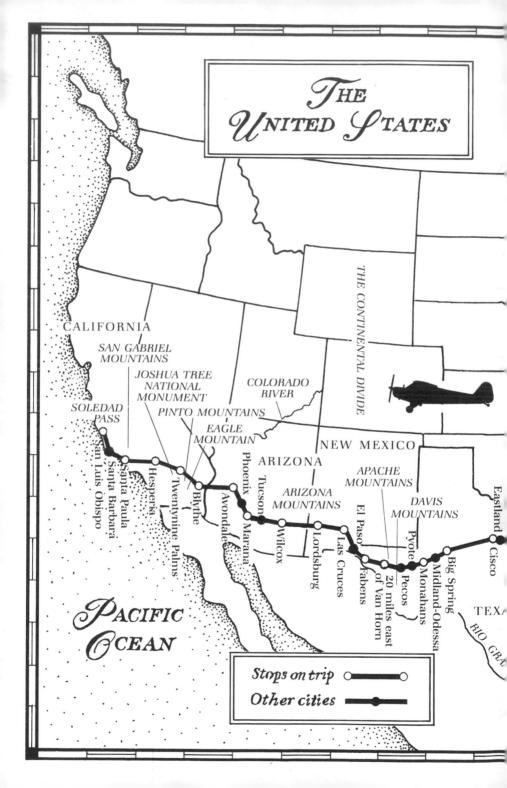